I0724289

THE OUTLANDS SHIFTER

Other Books by Anna Durand

The Outlands Demon (The Devil's Outlands, Book One)
The Mortal Falls (Undercover Elementals, Book One)
The Mortal Fires (Undercover Elementals, Book Two)
The Mortal Tempest (Undercover Elementals, Book Three)
The Janusite Trilogy (Undercover Elementals, Books 1-3)
Obsidian Hunger (Undercover Elementals, Book Four)
Unbidden Hunger (Undercover Elementals, Book Five)
The Thirteenth Fae (Undercover Elementals, Book Six)
Cyneric (Undercover Elementals, Book Seven)
Echo Power (Echo Power Trilogy, Book One)
Echo Dominion (Echo Power Trilogy, Book Two)
Echo Unbound (Echo Power Trilogy, Book Three)
Willpower (Psychic Crossroads, Book One)
Intuition (Psychic Crossroads, Book Two)
Kinetic (Psychic Crossroads, Book Three)
Passion Never Dies: The Complete Reborn Series
Banished in the Highlands (A Hot Scots Prequel)
The Notorious Dr. MacT (A Hot Scots Prequel)
The British Bastard (A Hot Scots Prequel)
The MacTaggart Brothers Trilogy (Hot Scots, Books 1-3)
Gift-Wrapped in a Kilt (Hot Scots, Book Four)
Notorious in a Kilt (Hot Scots, Book Five)
Insatiable in a Kilt (Hot Scots, Book Six)
Lethal in a Kilt (Hot Scots, Book Seven)
Irresistible in a Kilt (Hot Scots, Book Eight)
Devastating in a Kilt (Hot Scots, Book Nine)
Spellbound in a Kilt (Hot Scots, Book Ten)
Relentless in a Kilt (Hot Scots, Book Eleven)
Incendiary in a Kilt (Hot Scots, Book Twelve)
Wild in a Kilt (Hot Scots, Book Thirteen)
Brit vs. Scot (A Hot Brits/Hot Scots/Au Naturel Crossover Book)
The American Wives Club (A Hot Brits/Hot Scots/Au Naturel Crossover Book)
A Novel Secret (A Hot Brits/Hot Scots/Au Naturel Crossover Book)
The Dixon Brothers Trilogy (Hot Brits, Books 1-3)
One Hot Escape (Hot Brits, Book Four)
One Hot Rumor (Hot Brits, Book Five)
One Hot Christmas (Hot Brits, Book Six)
One Hot Scandal (Hot Brits, Book Seven)
One Hot Deal (Hot Brits, Book Eight)
One Hot Favor (Hot Brits, Book Nine)
One Hot Bash (Hot Brits, Book 10)
Natural Obsession (Au Naturel Nights, Book One)
Natural Deception (Au Naturel Nights, Book Two)
Natural Passion (Au Naturel Trilogy, Book One)
Natural Impulse (Au Naturel Trilogy, Book Two)
Natural Satisfaction (Au Naturel Trilogy, Book Three)
Fired Up (standalone romance)

THE OUTLANDS SHIFTER

The Devil's Outlands, Book One

ANNA DURAND

JACOBSVILLE BOOKS · MARIETTA, OHIO

THE OUTLANDS SHIFTER

Copyright © 2021 by Lisa A. Shiel
All rights reserved.

The characters and events in this book are fictional. No portion of this book may be copied, reproduced, or transmitted in any form or by any means, electronic or otherwise, including recording, photocopying, or inclusion in any information storage and retrieval system, without the express written permission of the publisher and author, except for brief excerpts quoted in published reviews.

ISBN: 978-1-949406-58-0 (paperback)
ISBN: 978-1-949406-59-7 (ebook)
ISBN: 978-1-949406-60-3 (audiobook)

Manufactured in the United States.

Jacobsville Books
www.JacobsvilleBooks.com

Publisher's Cataloging-in-Publication Data
provided by Five Rainbows Cataloging Services

Names: Durand, Anna.
Title: The outlands shifter / Anna Durand.
Description: Marietta, OH : Jacobsville Books, 2021.
Identifiers: ISBN 978-1-949406-58-0 (paperback) | ISBN 978-1-949406-59-7 (ebook) | ISBN 978-1-949406-60-3 (audiobook)
Subjects: LCSH: Werewolves--Fiction. | Shapeshifting--Fiction. | Time travel--Fiction. | Magic--Fiction. | British--Fiction. | Romance fiction. | BISAC: FICTION / Romance / Paranormal / Shifters. | FICTION / Romance / Time Travel. | FICTION / Romance / Historical / Victorian. | GSAFD: Love stories. | Occult fiction.
Classification: LCC PS3604.U724 O98 2021 (print) | LCC PS3604.U724 (ebook) | DDC 813/.6--dc23.

CHAPTER ONE

Kylie

Y ER DEAD, YA LILY-LIVERED THIEF!" THE COWBOY SHOUTS. HE SHAKES his fists in the air and bares his teeth like a wild animal. But he's not an animal. He's an actor playing a part.

I sigh as my gaze wanders over the street of the hokiest tourist trap in the Old West. At twenty bucks a pop, Wrathrock Ghost Town promises "a fantastic adventure through the mists of time with authentic Utah Old West flavor," but it delivers off-off-Broadway schlock. I once again scan the dusty dirt street that stretches for three blocks ahead of me, taking in the old-looking buildings lined up along either side of the road, buildings that might actually be old structures or might be artfully aged replicas. A block away, a stagecoach—the one my friends and I arrived in—waits in front of a building labeled "Sassy May's Boarding House."

Mopping sweat from my brow, I search the surroundings for anyplace where I might hunt down a bottle of water or a can of pop to quench my parched mouth. The midsummer sun scorches my skin and squeezes perspiration from every pore on my body. The sweat oozes down the back of my neck and between my breasts. Why did I wear a denim shirt over my tank top? Sure, the denim top is unbuttoned, but that doesn't make me feel any cooler.

I shrug out of the denim shirt and tie the sleeves around my waist. At least I had the good sense to wear shorts.

My attention wanders back to the phony cowboy.

He yanks the trigger on his clumsy, oversize revolver. The shot booms, echoing down the dusty street, while the other man, aka the lily-livered thief, lets out a melodramatic cry before collapsing in an exaggerated fall that sends his feet flying up as his backside hits the dirt.

The other tourists gathered before the duo cheer and clap. The faux cowboy proudly brandishes his gun over his head and smiles at the crowd. The "corpse" on the ground waves to the audience too, spoiling his ever-so-convincing act of playing dead.

"That was so lame," my best friend, Jenna Foster, mutters.

I look at Jenna, who's rolling her eyes at the previously deceased thief as he rises from the ground and takes a bow.

Jenna groans. "I mean, really, if these guys are SAG members, they should be kicked out for crimes against acting."

My other best friend, Megan Rivera, announces, "They can't be members, unless SAG stands for Sawdust Amateurs Guild."

"Oh, you two," I moan, returning my attention to the cowboys. "Drama students should not visit tourist traps. What did you expect, Shakespeare in the Park?"

Movement just past the two cowboys catches my eye, and I squint at the figure who walks out of the shadows beneath the saloon's porch. The man saunters into the street, his head turned away, a long and battered leather coat billowing around his legs and a rust-brown cowboy hat slanted low over his eyes. He towers over the two hams who are yucking it up for the crowd despite being several feet behind them. Just as the mysterious newcomer strides past the duo, he vanishes.

I stare at the space where he'd been. The guy had just...faded into nothing. Like a ghost.

A shiver tingles through me. I can't disguise the wonder in my voice when I say, "Wow, that was one amazing special effect. Did you guys see it?"

"See what?" Jenna asks as she tosses her hair over her shoulder.

I gesture past the cowboys. "The man who walked across the street behind those two and disappeared. How'd they do that?" I raise onto my tiptoes but can't see anything behind the cowboys. "Must've been a projection or a hologram or something."

"What man?" Megan asks, a hint of annoyance in her tone. "I was staring right in that direction, and nobody was there."

"He *was* there. I swear it." How could my friends have missed that imposing figure? Imposing and sexy. "I saw a guy with big muscles and wide shoulders wearing a wicked-cool leather coat."

Megan pats my shoulder. "Girl, you're majorly stressed about your capstone project, aren't you? Imagining hotties in a ghost town?" She leans closer to murmur in my ear, "You need to get laid, Kylie. Virginicity isn't good for your mental state."

"Virginicity is not a word."

"Sure it is." Megan straightens and smirks, eying the cowboys. "It's in the dictionary, right after Very Pent-Up Grad Student."

"I am not pent-up." When my friends giggle at my proclamation, I give up. If I hadn't known them both since fifth grade, I might take offense. But sarcasm is how we've always rolled, and I know my friends tease me because they love me. Maybe I did imagine that man. I'm thirsty, and dehydration can do weird things to a person. "I need a drink."

"Sorry, babe," Jenna says, nodding toward the saloon. "Family restaurant, no booze."

"I meant a drink of water."

Jenna grins and bumps her shoulder into mine. "I know. Just ribbing you. Could you please relax a little and try to get into the cheese factory we paid good money to see?" She adopts a fake pout that's a touch overdone. "I was hoping for sleazy cowboys who hit on saucy wenches in the crowd. Instead, we're stuck in Disneyland Meets the Dust Bowl."

"Let me get a drink and then we can leave. All right?"

Both Jenna and Megan voice their agreement, though not in actual words, and I sidle through the crowd to hop up onto the saloon porch. From this vantage, I have a better view of the mountains far beyond the ghost town's limits, their slopes rising high above the Great Basin, in which Wrath-rock lies. Though I've lived in this area for six years, since my best friends and I decided to escape rainy Seattle for the stunning scenery of west-central Utah, I still feel a little out of place here. For as long as I can remember, I've searched for a sense of connection that I never quite find.

Connection. What a silly idea. An ornithology grad student, steeped in science, ought to be immune to sappy mumbo-jumbo. Not that I'll ever admit to Jenna or Megan that I yearn for something I can't define, a nebulous need beyond my reach.

And yes, there are birds in this arid region.

I buy a can of Pepsi from a vending machine inside the saloon and amble to the end of the porch, near where I saw—or thought I saw—the man in the leather coat. While the two lame-ass cowboys left footprints on the dirt street, the path my mystery man took is clean. *Because he doesn't exist, moron.* Too many hours of studying the migration patterns of the cliff swallow must've fried my brain.

A scuffling noise draws my attention to the shadow-cloaked alley between the saloon and the general store. My breath catches, and my pulse quickens.

The man in the leather coat strides down the alley away from me.

I leap off the porch, rocketing down the alley after him, but he's already swerving around a corner into another alley behind the general store. I veer around the corner, stumbling to a halt when I realize the alley ends a few yards ahead of me. Panting, my heart pounding, I swipe the sweat from my brow with the back of my hand.

The man is gone, of course. Hallucinations tend to vanish without a trace.

Why can't I meet a guy like that? A real man, not a wuss like all the guys I've met who aren't hallucinations. Is it too much to ask for a hero who takes my breath away? Or at least doesn't wear baggy cargo pants? I long for the kind of man I've read about in books and seen in old movies, the kind who kisses a woman like he means it.

Oh jeez. Maybe I do need to get laid after all.

I've still got the unopened Pepsi can in my hand. So I pop the top, take a sip, and survey the ground for footprints. Nothing but my tracks. I swig more pop, and the blessed chill of it feels so good even while the carbonation sizzles down my throat. I toss back another mouthful, letting my eyes drift shut.

Someone coughs.

My lids fly open.

I gasp at the old man who hunches before me, leaning on a gnarled wooden walking stick. He studies me, his ink-dark eyes squinted. Wrinkles carve deep lines on his face while a sharp, hooked nose lends him the noble air of a bald eagle. A woven poncho covers his bent frame, and gray hair flares wildly around his head.

"There you are," he says, his voice brittle. "I've been waiting for you, Kylie."

I stagger backward half a step. Waiting for me? No, that's not creepy at all. "How do you know my name?"

"Been waiting for you," he repeats, as if that explains everything. "Took so much longer than I anticipated, but fate has a way of meandering to its destination."

Since I have no clue what the man is babbling about, I decide it's time to exit the conversation. I back up a few more steps, then whirl around and lurch into a dead run.

And I smack into the old man.

I stumble backward, and the pop can flies out of my grasp. It plops onto the dirt, spewing brown liquid.

The old man raises a placating hand.

My pulse thunders in my ears anyway. "How did you..."

"The old ways." He shuts his eyes briefly. "I have no time to explain, dear, else I would. But the winds of time speak your name, and nothing can stop what must come to pass."

A warm breeze tickles my midriff, and I realize with a start that my tank top had ridden up when I'd stumbled into the old man. Yanking it down, I tuck the hem under the denim shirt that's still tied around my waist. "I have no clue what you're talking about."

"You will soon." He reaches inside his poncho to pull out a bronze medallion the size of a silver dollar that hangs from a thick cord fashioned from what looks like hemp. "This is yours."

He removes the necklace and holds it out to me.

I stare at the medallion and its frayed cord. Taking gifts from strangers was one of the big no-no's I learned as a child. But I'm an adult now, right? Twenty-four and capable of taking care of myself. Besides, what harm can a medallion do?

The old man jiggles the necklace. "Take it, child. You will need its power soon."

"Power?"

My gaze locks onto the medallion as the bronze disk rotates on its axis, revealing flashes of both sides. One face has a five-pointed star on it, while the other features a stylized image of a howling wolf. It doesn't look Native American, though I'm hardly an expert. The medallion seems more Old World European.

"Who are you?" I ask.

"A shaman of sorts. My people once lived in the lands that encompass this place." He shakes his head, his face pinched and his eyes half-closed as if he's recalling a painful memory. "The curse will not let go. The Old Ones have spoken, and it was your name they called." His eyes spring open, fixed on me with an unnerving intensity that sends a shiver wriggling down my spine. "Kylie Drummond, the purest soul and keeper of the wolf's destiny."

Another shiver rakes down my spine, harder this time, and goosebumps pebble my arms. Wolf's destiny? Purest soul? It's a bunch of wacko nonsense.

"Yeah, sure," I tell him. "Whatever you say."

He swings the necklace side to side like a pendulum. "Your life will change when you embrace the power of the medallion."

The eerie way he intones those words does something strange to me. My mind is fuzzy, my pulse has slowed, and I can't move a muscle or look away from his eyes. I stretch out a trembling hand and close it around the medallion, feeling its cool metal against my palm. The second my hand encloses the disk, a gust of wind blows dust into my eyes, forcing me to shut them tight. When I peel them open again, the old man is gone.

But I still clasp the medallion in my palm.

I stand here frozen, dumbfounded by what I think I experienced. Am I suffering from heat-induced hallucinations? The warmth of my palm leeches into the bronze disk, which seems to amplify the temperature until it almost burns my skin. I open my hand and let the medallion dangle from its hemp cord. The metal reflects the sunlight, though its tarnished surface dulls the effect.

A lump hardens in my throat. I swallow, but that lump won't budge.

Okay, not a hallucination. Unless I've sunk so far into the deep end that I can't tell reality from fantasy anymore. The medallion swings side to side, over and over, the image of the wolf moving with it. The bronze disk commands my focus and, unable to tear my gaze away, I let my eyes shift left, right, left, right, in time with the medallion.

The world tilts around me.

A wave of dizziness crashes over me, and I stagger sideways, flailing for a handhold but finding none. My right hand still clutches the medallion's cord, so tight that my knuckles ache and my nails dig into my palm. The spinning sensation quickens, the world gyrating as if I've hopped onto one of those Tilt-A-Whirl rides at a carnival. Nausea surges in my stomach, the pressure of it forcing my gorge high in my throat. Oh God, I'm about to vomit.

I stumble out of the alley, careening like a drunken cowboy, my vision suddenly blurred. Darkness envelops me. An impulse too strong to deny compels me onward through total blackness while my heart hammers in my chest. Adrenaline scorches through my veins, and I know it's the only thing keeping me on my feet. A seductive abyss beckons me. I recognize that if I give in to the abyss, I'll fall to the ground unconscious, vulnerable to whatever the hell is happening to me.

I bump into a barrier, lose my balance, and slump to my knees in the dirt, breathless, my ears ringing.

"There she is!"

"Oh my God! Kylie!"

Familiar voices pull me out of the viscous blackness that gropes at my flesh. My vision lightens, and blurry shapes coalesce into people and objects. Jenna and Megan are racing toward me from the other side of the ghost town's main street, followed close behind by a bald man I don't recognize.

I blink slowly, drawing one deep breath after another. Where am I? On the ground, I realize, crouched at the end of the saloon's porch. When I tip my head back, I can see the porch railing.

"Are you okay?" Megan asks, her voice fraught with anxiety. She drops to her knees beside me. "We were totally freaked out. Where'd you go?"

Jenna kneels in front of me, her eyes wide, her face pale. "Girl, where have you been? You scared us half to death, disappearing like that."

"What?" I say, still too dazed to understand anything. I rub my temples, but my friends' reactions seem out of proportion. "I was only gone a few minutes."

"Minutes?" Jenna says. "You disappeared for three freaking hours, Kylie."

Hours? No, it can't have been that long. I glance over my shoulder at the alley—which is not there. No more than a few feet separates the saloon from the general store, and another structure backs up to the buildings I'm crouched between right now. *No alley.*

A bone-deep chill penetrates me down to my soul.

"Don't you remember anything?" Jenna asks.

I shake my head. Sure, I remember stuff—but nothing I can admit to remembering. They'll think I've gone bonkers. "I could swear it was only a few minutes."

"We're getting you the hell out of this place."

Megan and Jenna seize my arms, urging me to get up. Jenna hooks her arm around mine while Megan does the same on the other side of me. Supported by my friends, I let them lead me out into the street, to where the bald man stands wringing his hands.

"Ms. Drummond," he says, "I'm Al Bridger, the manager here. We've been searching for you for hours. Nothing like this has ever happened before in the whole history of Wrathrock Ghost Town. Please accept our sincerest apologies."

I manage a weak smile. "I must've gotten dehydrated and wandered off. It's my fault."

"We have a medic on staff." Bridger waves toward the boarding house. "Let me give you a room here, and our medic can take a look at you."

"No thanks." The mere thought of sticking around here makes me uneasy. And yet, I feel a strange thrill at the prospect too. "I just want to leave. I'm okay, promise."

"Then may I give you girls a ride back into town? I have a Land Rover. It's much more comfortable than the stagecoach."

I nod, letting him know I'm cool with that idea. Another bumpy, bone-rattling ride in the quaint stagecoach does not appeal to me. Shaking off my friends' arms, I trail Al Bridger down the street, between two buildings, and into a parking area where a Land Rover awaits. Soon, I'll be back in my nice cool hotel room. Tomorrow, we will all head back to the university, and I can immerse myself in ornithology again, forgetting this freaky day ever happened.

A gust of wind blusters past me, whipping my hair around my face. I lift a hand to brush it away.

The medallion dangles from my fingers.

"Where did you get that?" Megan asks, pointing at the bronze disk. "And what on earth is it?"

I swallow hard and stuff the thing in my pocket. "It's nothing. Nothing at all."

CHAPTER TWO

Kylie

I LIE FLAT ON MY BACK, ARMS AT MY SIDES, FINGERS DRUMMING ON THE blanket. My mind refuses to calm down and let me get some rest. In the big bed next to mine, Jenna snores softly, and Megan mumbles in her sleep. I'd volunteered to crash on a foldaway bed since the hotel had been booked up, except for one available room which has a single queen-size bed. Jenna had offered me one of her sleeping pills, saying I must need it after my "freaky ordeal." I declined her offer. Taking a pill won't erase what I experienced back in Wrathrock. I still feel...weird.

So yeah, it looks like no sleep for me tonight.

My mind keeps replaying it all in ultra-HD clarity. The cowboy in the wicked-cool leather coat. The muscles I could just make out under his clothes. That equally awesome hat. He'd looked like the quintessential Wild West outlaw, strong and virile and sexy as hell.

Except he was a hallucination.

My skin itches like I've brushed against poison ivy or something. I haven't, though, and this itch feels unlike anything caused by skin irritation. It prickles deep under the surface. I try not to scratch, but the sensation gets stronger and itchier, and I need to scrape my nails on my skin, need it so badly that I'm squirming and gritting my teeth. I fist my hands over my belly and take slow, deep breaths while I will the itching to stop. This room has gotten stuffy, which always makes my skin prickly. That must be the reason for it, though I've never had this strong a reaction to a stuffy room before.

I swing my feet off the bed, slipping them into my plaid slippers. The silky blue fabric of my short satin nightie slides over my skin as I push up off the bed. One of the spaghetti straps falls off my shoulder, and I push it back into place. A faint draft teases my skin from mid-thigh down to my ankles, and on my shoulders and arms too, eliciting goosebumps.

How can I get cold right after realizing the stuffy room is making me itchy?

The draft whispers over me, around me, through me, like a ghost trying to touch me and make contact. Bullshit. I'm still in the grips of a mental freak-out, that's all.

But I don't feel freaked out.

Searching the dimly lit room, I spot my robe where I'd left it draped over the foot of the bed. Shrugging it on, I tie the belt and pad over to the window. In the glow of the moon, I can see the other buildings nearby. Our room sits on the backside of the hotel where the sulfurous illumination of the streetlights in the parking lot can't reach. Vacant scrubland stretches away from the hotel toward the dark, hulking shapes of the mountains in the distance.

The chill I felt a minute ago has vanished.

And my skin itches again.

I grasp the window sash with both hands and thrust it upward. Thank goodness this is an older hotel that still has windows that open. Cool night air wafts over and around me, kissing my arms and my throat, chilling my lips. The moon hangs high in the sky, full and bright. If I got out my binoculars, I'm sure I could make out all the big geologic features on the moon. I plant my palms on the windowsill, leaning into them, and inhale a lungful of fresh air.

A wolf's howl echoes across the landscape, distant but clear, full of a longing that stabs a pain into my chest.

Oh come on. Now I'm getting emotional about a wolf howling? *Sheesh, girl, maybe you should take that sleeping pill after all.*

The wolf howls again, the mournful sound stretching on and on until it finally fades away.

A tingle rushes over my skin, raising every hair on my body. *Find him.*

The voice that whispers the command into my mind is not my voice. Something outside of me has crept in to whisper in my thoughts. It's crazy. *I* must be crazy. But the wolf's call has burrowed inside me so deep that it touches my soul. I need to find that beast. Right now.

No, no, no, I'm not crazy enough to do that. Absolutely not.

Another howl echoes across the landscape.

Find him.

I can't resist the call any longer. Something overtakes me, like a wild spirit has possessed me, and I can't stop my feet from carrying me out of the room. I grab the medallion the shaman gave me and drop it into the pocket of my robe while I tiptoe out the door, easing it shut so the latch makes only the barest of clicks. Then I race down the stairs, because the elevator would take too damn long, and fly down the first-floor hallway to the side door. By the time the door shuts, I'm barreling down the main street, out of town and into the night that's lit only by the moon's glow.

Suddenly, I stop. Breathing hard, my pulse racing, I glance around. Where am I going? The nearest place is Wrathrock, but the ghost town is half a mile away. Running, or even walking, that far in fuzzy plaid slippers seems like total insanity.

The wolf howls again.

I can't fight the impulse. It itches deep inside me, and I have no choice. The spirit possessing me takes control again, propelling me to gallop down the dirt road, my arms and legs pumping, my lungs burning. *Get there, hurry, get there.* Sweat streams down my temples, dampens my hair, and trickles between my breasts. And still, I cannot stop.

At the edge of the ghost town, I stumble to a halt. I'm breathing so hard my ears have started to ring, and I wobble slightly from the wooziness brought on by my desperate flight. Okay, I'm here. Now what?

The world tilts around me like one of those carnival rides, the way it had earlier when I'd seen—*thought* I'd seen—the mysterious cowboy. This time, the world keeps tilting more and more wildly until it's whirling around me so fast that I can't see through the spinning blur. My stomach lurches, shooting bile up into my throat. Wind erupts around me, lashing my hair to my face, and an unearthly roar deafens me. My legs buckle. I hit the ground hard, pain spiking through my knees, my breathing so hectic that I might be hyperventilating.

And I collapse face-first onto the dirt street of Wrathrock.

How long I'm out, I don't know. My long journey back toward consciousness starts with my ears. I hear unfamiliar voices saying things I can't make out at first, then my brain finally remembers how to interpret words.

"Is she dead?"

"Nah. Look, Silas, her eyes are movin'."

Something nudges me. A foot, maybe?

"Yer right, Arlo," the first voice says. "She ain't dead. But where'd she come from?"

"Don't know. The way she's dressed, she's gotta be a saloon girl."

The other person—man?—grunts. "His Highness didn't say he got a new girl. And why in tarnation is she out here flat on the ground?"

"Girl's drunk as a skunk, that's why."

I hear a sniffing sound near my ear, then one of the men speaks close to my face. "She ain't drunk. Smells like woman stuff. Parfoom water or somethin'."

"Get away from her!" shouts another voice, one farther away and much deeper. The man speaks with an authoritative tone as if he's used to people doing whatever he says. There's something odd about his voice, but I can't quite figure it out.

Scuffling suggests the two men who'd been examining me have moved away.

My muscles decide to start functioning again, so I open my eyes and heave myself into a sitting position. My legs are bent under me, and I need to keep a hand on the ground for support. Whatever happened, it's left me shaky. I blink swiftly until my vision clears.

Light emanates from the buildings that line the street, revealing the men who have gathered around me. Two scruffy-looking men in rumpled cowboy-type clothes stand to one side of me, eying me like I'm a fresh side of beef they want to cook up and devour.

A third man, who must be the one who shouted at the other two, saunters up to me and tips his head side to side like he's studying me. The light behind him casts his front in shadow. His hat shades his face, so I can't make out his features.

"What have you done?" he snarls at the other two.

"Nothin'. We heard a noise, turned around, and there she was."

The man with the authoritative voice angles slightly to the side to glare at the other two. Light spills over his face.

My jaw drops. *Holy shit.* It's the mysterious cowboy I'd seen this afternoon, the one who vanished into thin air. I hadn't seen his face the first time, but I recognize his clothes and the way he carries himself, not to mention his muscles. This can mean only one thing. I've gone certifiably insane.

The man in the wicked-cool leather coat kneels in front of me, his gray eyes narrowed and his mouth compressed into a hard slash. His light-brown hair is mostly hidden under his hat.

He sweeps his gaze over my entire body.

My robe has fallen open, and my nightie has ridden up so it barely covers my privates.

The mystery man's tongue glides across his lower lip. His nostrils flare. He shuts his eyes for a heartbeat, then aims his steely gaze at me. "How did you get here?"

"I-I don't know. I started walking from town and then I got dizzy, and I woke up here."

"You *are* in town," he says. "Where did you come from?"

My brain, at last, realizes what's odd about his voice and relays the information to me. He has a British accent.

The way he's staring at me shivers warmth through me even while I feel like scrambling away from him. "I came from the university. My friends and I thought it might be fun to see the ghost town. I-I don't know how I got here, and I had no idea anybody worked in this park at night." He keeps staring at me with that hard expression for so long that I feel the need to tug my robe closed to cover myself. "Sorry if I interrupted your show."

The man leans in so close that his nose almost brushes mine. He sniffs once, then pulls in a big breath through his nostrils.

And he growls.

The sound is soft and probably not noticeable to anybody else, but I heard it. This guy growled. Seriously.

He grabs my arms and gets up, hoisting me up with him. With his hands around my wrists, he pulls me close. "You don't belong here, little girl. But since you have deigned to enter my domain, you belong to me." He flashes the hottest glare I've ever seen at the other men. "Go back to the hellhole you call home, both of you."

A crowd of men and women pour out of a building I suddenly realize is the saloon. They all freeze when they see me and the man who has me in his clutches.

He slings an arm around my waist, crushing me to his hard body, and scans the crowd. Then he hollers, "No one will touch this woman. She is my property. Understand?"

Murmurs and nodding heads indicate they get it.

I gaze up at the man to whose body I'm plastered. I feel every one of his muscles. "Who are you?"

"Sheriff Nathaniel Fortescue."

"My name is Kylie." I swallow, but the tightness in my throat lingers. "Kylie Drummond. Where am I?"

He bends his head closer to mine, his stubble rasping against my cheek. "You are in the Devil's Outlands, little girl. Better known as Hell on earth."

CHAPTER THREE

Nathaniel

WHAT AM I DOING WITH THIS WOMAN? I WOULD PREFER TO STAY away from her, but I have no choice in the matter. Now that the townsfolk have seen her, she will become prey. Yes, she might be prey to me too, but unlike the miscreants around us, I won't rip her to pieces for the pleasure of it. I have only one choice to save this strange girl's life.

I sweep her into my arms and march toward the saloon, straight through the swinging doors, past the bar and the patrons seated on stools or at tables. Every drunken face jerks up to stare at us. Some of the men sneer and snigger. The few women in this den of debauchery scowl or smirk. They will be quite annoyed with me, but I have less than a thought to spare for their ilk. The opinions of whores and blackguards mean nothing to me.

"Put me down," says the woman in my arms. She wriggles but can't get free. "I said put me down, you caveman."

I've been called much worse. If she intended to wound me, she will need to choose much sharper words than that.

"Silence, child," I snarl as I stomp up the stairs.

The girl crosses her arms over her chest. "You are so rude. And my name is Kylie, not 'child,' so please stop calling me that."

I have never heard the name Kylie before. It sounds like a boy's pet name.

She kicks her feet, so I lock my arm around her knees. Lips puckered, eyes narrowed, she tries to beat me with her little fists. I roll her toward me so her arms are pinned between our bodies.

"Give up the struggle," I hiss under my breath. "You cannot escape me."

The creature in my arms sinks her teeth into my nose.

I bite back a curse as I charge down the hallway to the only room where I can safely house her. She will not appreciate the accommodations, I'm certain of that, but she will have no say in the matter. Unlocking the door requires me to set her down, though I keep my arm barred around her with her arms crushed between us. I extract the key from my pocket and insert it into the lock.

"What kind of funky key is that?" she asks.

I clench my teeth. "Will you cease speaking?"

"No, I will not. Excuse me for getting pissy when I'm being abducted by a caveman."

There is no chance she will stop spouting bizarre words, is there? I haven't a clue what "pissy" means, though perhaps she thinks I plan to urinate on her.

Still holding her to my side, I hoist her off her feet and carry the creature inside the room, kicking the door shut. The oil lantern I always leave burning casts flickering tongues of illumination through the room. I deposit the creature on the bed. Her dark-brown hair falls over her face, and she blows it away. Her garments, the smallest I've ever seen, slide up almost to her hips. I glimpse dark, curly hairs at the juncture of her thighs.

And I growl low in my throat.

The girl gathers her brows over her nose, drawing my attention to her green eyes and the golden highlights in them. "Are you seriously growling at me? I guess you're nothing but a dirty dog."

I lean in and growl again. "No, child, I am a wolf."

She huffs. "Please. I've dealt with worse creeps than you."

Her dressing gown has fallen off one shoulder, revealing creamy, smooth skin. I can see her breasts too, though not the peaks that jut under the fabric of her nightgown or whatever the garment is meant to be. It has the slenderest straps I've ever seen. Has the devil himself sent this creature to tempt me into selling him my soul? He's too late. My soul has been claimed by a different beast.

I can't resist sliding a finger under the slender strap of her garment, then gliding it up and down. The sensation of her soft skin brushing mine makes my cock throb and the beast within me awaken. I must go. Now.

But I need to know more about this creature who appeared seemingly from nowhere and who has become my charge, regardless of whether I want dominion over her.

Perhaps I do want that, more than I should.

I take two steps backward. "Where did you come from?"

"Fiara Flats. It's half a mile down the road."

My blood freezes, and for a heartbeat, the room seems to spin. "There is no such town."

But I know what those words mean. It cannot be, yet it is. Beast Flats. The first part of the name means "beast" in Romanian. She claims to hail from Fiara Flats, but no such place exists. Why would she lie? Perhaps the town was recently founded.

Even if that's the case, it cannot have anything to do with my past.

"What's wrong with you?" she asks. "Are you about to barf?"

I stare at her, unable to produce a single word for a moment that feels like forever. What language does this child speak? I know Americans speak a bizarre version of English, but I've not heard anyone speak the sort of words this creature spouts.

She puckers her lips while she examines me with her gaze. "You don't look anything like the British guys I've seen on TV. I mean, you're a cowboy. That's freaky. Prince William doesn't growl, as far as I know, but don't even get me started on Prince Harry."

I understood only a fraction of the syllables she uttered. Perhaps she escaped from an insane asylum, and that's why her words sound like gibberish.

England has no Prince William or Prince Harry, and I'm not aware of America having any royalty. Perhaps she refers to honorary titles.

"From what country do these princes hail?" I ask.

"Where do you think? England, like you. Duh."

Yes, she is clearly insane. An asylum escapee seems the most plausible explanation for...her.

I lean in until our noses are a hair's breadth apart. "I was once a member of the peerage, and there is no Prince William or Prince Harry in England."

She peers into my eyes. "Do you have amnesia? Is that why you're pretending to be a cowboy? Or maybe you're not really British. Your scrambled brain thinks you are."

What in the name of all that's holy is this creature saying?

The girl wrinkles her nose. "Peerage? What's that?"

"It means I was titled, once upon a time. I was the Earl of Wilderhampton."

"Ohhh, I get it. You're one of *those* Brits. Why aren't you an earl anymore?"

"That is none of your concern." I force myself to step away from her. The beast within has already awakened, and the scent of her is rousing its hunger. But I feel an incomprehensible need to cow this feminine creature, so I speak in the most condescending tone I can marshal. "Ah yes, you're one of *those* Americans. I suppose you must be royalty, considering your arrogant behavior."

She rolls her eyes. "Oh yeah, I'm the Queen of Disneyland."

"I am unfamiliar with a kingdom called Disneyland. Where is it located?"

"Anaheim, California."

Well, at least I know where California is.

The girl takes a deep breath, which lifts her breasts.

I swallow a growl. "You will remain here until I return."

"When will that be?"

"Morning." I spin around and stalk to the door, but as I grasp the knob, I hear the infernal woman's voice.

"Why are there bars on the windows?"

I rush out the door and slam it shut.

My footfalls pound on the stairs as I make my way down to the saloon, heading for the front entrance. The call is pulling at me already, and though the moon is not quite full tonight, I still need to get away from town to be certain these people, however vile they might be, will suffer no harm. I've tried ordering them to stay indoors, but hiding won't protect them.

I would lock myself in the room upstairs, but I've had to give that space to the strange and most likely insane woman who appeared out of nowhere.

As I step off the last stair, Lucy stops wiping the set of glasses she'd been cleaning. "Well, if it ain't Lord Wolfie hisself. Where ya goin' now?"

"My whereabouts are none of your concern."

"What about that sweet little thang you just locked up in your dungeon?"

"Mind your mouth, Lucy, before I silence you myself."

She resumes cleaning the glasses, her head down, though she glances up at me as I stalk past the bar and out of the saloon.

The moon hangs low in the sky, squatting just above the roofs of the buildings. Its pull tugs at me, and I need every measure of willpower I possess to stave off what I know will come, whether I wish it or not. My skin crawls as if spiders with talons of acid have infested my skin. I break into a run, barreling down the street and out of town, into the barren environs beyond the limits of human habitation. The moment I've traveled beyond the sight of anyone in town, I halt and catch my breath.

Then I strip off all my clothes.

CHAPTER FOUR

Kylie

I PACE BACK AND FORTH IN MY LOVELY LITTLE CELL, WONDERING what kind of twisted dream or practical joke I'm experiencing right now. Why are there bars on the windows? I'd asked Nathaniel, Earl of Whatever-hampton, but he ignored my question. Big surprise. He might be hot, but he's the rudest, most obnoxious man I've ever met. So much for Brits always being polite.

He left me in here without any explanation or apology.

And half-naked too. Well, not quite half-naked. My nightie is skimpy, though, and my robe stops halfway down my thighs. It's chilly in here, and my feet are getting cold despite the slippers I'm wearing. I wrap my robe around myself and tie it shut with a knot. Then I wander over to the door and try the knob. Locked, of course. I'd heard Nathaniel lock it. But a girl has to try, right?

I lay my palm on the door. The surface is cool, rough metal.

What does he do in this room that requires unbreakable walls?

Since I have nothing else to do, I walk the perimeter of the room while skimming my fingers over it as I go. Every wall is composed of metal like the door, though it's covered up with plain brown wallpaper. I can tell the wallpaper hides a metal surface, though, because no wood is as hard as what lies under the plain brown exterior. I find a spot where the wallpaper has peeled up just a touch, enough for me to slide a fingernail under it and feel the metal surface beneath. I bet it's iron.

Perfect. I'm trapped in an ironclad room with barred windows and no way out. The wood floor probably has metal underneath it too.

This must be a dream. Or a trick. It can't be real.

As I'm nearing one of the two windows in this room, my fingertips graze over more tears in the wallpaper. I stop to examine the damage. It doesn't look like the paper just peeled off. No, it looks an awful lot like scratches made by... claws. Too big for a house cat, and also too high up for that.

Jeez, this place gives me the creeps.

I approach the window and gaze out through the bars. People mill around in the street, and though I can hear their voices through the glass, I can't make out their words. My attention wanders past the buildings to the landscape beyond.

Not a thing in sight. Just mountains, scrubland, and a dusty two-track that disappears into the distance where scrub gives way to desert.

But the ghost town isn't far from the hotel where my friends and I stayed last night. There's a city beyond that and a ski resort in the mountains that I could see from the hotel-room window. And what about the roads? The interstate? The university campus?

I see none of that.

Either this is the most outrageously realistic tourist trap ever, complete with giant screens to display a desolate landscape and hide the modern stuff in the distance, or...

No. Oh no, no, no. I'm not crazy enough to believe that. It's impossible.

I've been drugged. Yeah, that's it. Nathaniel or one of his buddies dosed me with something. Without using any needles or spraying anything in my face. I never took any pills, for sure. Well, unless somebody shoved one down my throat while I was unconscious, but I don't feel drugged.

There's no way. It can't be what it seems to be.

I shuffle to the foot of the bed and park my butt on it, staring straight ahead at nothing. I remember meeting that weird shaman guy, almost passing out, going back to the hotel with my friends, watching the moon through the open window and hearing a wolf howl, then bolting down the dirt road toward the ghost town. When that bizarre dizziness hit, I'd passed out.

And then...

I woke up here. Surrounded by creepy cowboys who leered at me.

Until Nathaniel showed up and took me away. To his private prison cell for half-naked women.

Oh God, am I seriously admitting that I might have possibly, potentially, kind of...time-traveled? I thought HG Wells made that stuff up.

A shiver dances over my skin, raising the hairs on my arms and at my nape. My attention drifts to the floor, and I shuffle across it to study the strange patterns within the wood. No, not patterns. They're scars. I kneel near the most badly scarred section and run my fingers over the marks. Long, narrow gouges. They almost look like—

Claw marks. From a large animal.

I shudder from another, much fiercer wave of cold that sweeps through me. Why would Nathaniel lock an animal in here? That would explain the metal encasing this room, I guess, but that knowledge doesn't make me feel better.

The British cowboy sometimes growls at me. Like an animal. Does he lock himself in here? No, that's nuts. Sure, like everything else that's happened to me tonight isn't.

I can't just sit here. I need to escape, somehow.

From a metal-encased cell in the past. Sure, no problem. I'll make a shiv out of my nightie. Where's MacGyver when you need him? There are people downstairs. Sure, they're weird and creepy, but maybe one of them will let me out of here.

I march over to the door and bang my fists on it. "Help! Get me out of here! Help!"

Can anyone hear me? I have no idea how thick this door is, but my fists barely make any sound when I thump on the metal. I need something harder than my hands.

I glance around, my gaze landing on the small dresser beside the bed. Maybe I can pull out one of the drawers and bash that into the iron door to make noise. So I do that, tossing away clothes that look like they belong to a man, and pound the drawer against the door while screaming even louder than the first time.

"Quit your caterwauling," someone shouts from the other side of the door. "You're botherin' my customers."

The voice belongs to a woman, I'm sure. Is it too much to hope for a little sisterly solidarity?

"Please let me out," I say. "He locked me in here without any food or water."

"I ain't got the key. Better get some sleep because Lord Wolfie won't be back until dawn."

"Please, don't leave me in here. What if I need to use the toilet?" I don't see one in this room.

"Not my problem. What he wants, he gets. But I'll let his lordyship know you're wantin' a chamber pot."

Gee, thanks a bunch.

I hear footsteps receding.

She left me here. So much for sisterly solidarity.

Why did she call him Lord Wolfie? He was the Earl of Wilder-whatsit, but that doesn't sound like "wolf." He does growl, though...

Oh, whatever. I'm trapped in here for the night, so I might as well get comfortable.

I crawl under the sheets but leave the oil lamp burning. Darkness doesn't appeal to me right now. The bed has a large, ornate headboard plus a similar footboard, and it seems to have metal springs in it. The mattress feels cushier than I would've expected. The sheets are surprisingly soft too, and the quilt keeps me warm. I don't expect to sleep, but at some point, I doze off and dream about a wolf howling, the medallion shimmering in my hand, and the hot British cowboy who rescued me.

But I swear I rouse at some point, just enough to hear a real wolf baying.

I wake up just as sunrise is peeking over the horizon, on fire with shades of pink and purple. Something warm presses against my hip. I push the covers off me and pat my hip, feeling the hard outline of the medallion in the pocket of my robe. I pull it out, letting it dangle from the hemp cord, and stare at the image of the wolf engraved on the metal.

Footsteps pound outside the door, coming closer.

I scramble off the bed, stuffing the medallion back in my pocket, and tie my robe securely. *No more ogling my boobs, Mr. Earl of Rude-hampton.*

The sound of a key turning in the lock tells me Nathaniel Fortescue has deigned to return. He throws the door open, strides across the threshold, and shuts the door again. He's carrying a chamber pot.

"I've brought you this," he says, setting the pot on the floor. His gaze travels over my entire body. "You need clothing."

"Duh. What I need the most, though, is for you to let me go."

"I can't. It's not safe." He rakes his gaze over me again, slower this time, and rubs his jaw. "I've asked Lucy to find something for you to wear."

"Am I supposed to thank you for that?"

His attention swerves to my hip, and his brows crinkle. "What is in your pocket?"

"None of your business."

I glance down and realize the medallion's shape is visible inside my pocket. Last night, my robe had been hanging loose, and the billowing fabric must've camouflaged the metal disk in my pocket. This morning, I'd tied the robe tightly around myself. That's why the outline of the medallion is showing now.

"Everything about you is my business." He stomps up to me and shoves his hand into my pocket. "Are you hiding a gold coin in here?"

My breath hitches. The heat of his hand penetrates the satin fabric, warming my skin and making me tingle in the most inappropriate places.

"Get your hand out of my pocket," I say through clenched teeth. "Shouldn't an earl be concerned with propriety?"

"This is the Devil's Outlands. Propriety has no place here."

"Why is this town called the Devil's Outlands?"

"It has no name. The Outlands encompasses the town and the surrounding area for several miles in all directions."

"But why—"

"Silence." He moves his fingers inside my pocket, massaging in gentle circles. "I can do anything I want to you, and no one will lift a finger to stop me. This town belongs to me, and so do you."

"Like hell."

I ram my knee into his groin.

He grunts and stumbles backward. The movement rips his hand out of my pocket and sends the medallion tumbling to the floor.

Nathaniel stares at it, still doubled over.

I cross my arms. "Don't mess with me, Lord Jackass."

He rolls his eyes up to look at me. "Where did you get that medallion?"

"It was a gift."

"From whom?"

"Uh-uh. You don't get to interrogate me when you were sexually harassing me a few seconds ago."

He grabs the medallion and straightens, holding it up between us. "Where did you get this?"

"Don't remember."

"Lying to me is unwise, child."

"Maybe I'd be more cooperative if you stopped acting like a caveman."

He stuffs the medallion in his pocket. "Whether you choose to cooperate is irrelevant. You belong to me, and you will do as I say or suffer the consequences."

"If you try to rape me, I'll bite and kick and claw until you can't see through the blood coming out of your eyes and your dick."

"My what?"

"Your dick." I watch him, but he still seems confused by the word I used. So I wave toward his groin. "Your penis?"

He glances down at his body. Keeping his head bowed, he looks up at me. His voice sounds rougher and hungrier when he speaks. "I won't need to force my attentions on you. If I want to debauch you, I'll have you begging me to do it."

"In your dreams. *Never going to happen.*"

He winces and jerks.

And smoke starts to waft out of his pants pocket.

CHAPTER FIVE

Nathaniel

MY TROUSERS ARE ON FIRE. I TRY TO SHOVE MY HAND INTO MY POCK-et to pull out the medallion, which is burning through the fabric, but it scalds my skin the second I touch it. Snarling an oath, I tear my boots and socks off and remove my trousers as quickly as possible, stumbling sideways in the process. I succeed in shedding the garment before the medallion can incinerate the fabric and my skin.

I toss the ruined trousers onto the floor.

The girl is gaping at me.

No, not at me. She stares at my loins, her mouth open and her eyes wide.

I am naked from the waist down, though my shirt hangs low enough to conceal a portion of my loins. Let the child gape at me. I have more pressing matters to discuss with her, beginning with that medallion. I'd seen one identical to it, years ago. That other medallion hadn't burned me, but the agony it wrought had been far worse than what transpired a moment ago.

The girl's gaze repeatedly darts to my face, then back to my loins, while her cheeks grow pink. "I thought cowboys wore long johns. That's what movies told me."

Movies? Long johns? She's spouting nonsensical words again. "Perhaps you could attempt to speak proper English."

"I am, just not your version of it. Long johns are long underwear. And movies are...too hard to explain."

"Yes, I imagine it is difficult to explain nonsense. As for long underwear, I believe you are referring to union suits. I find them too warm for this climate."

I start to walk toward the dresser until I realize my clothes have been dumped on the floor and the drawer that had housed them lies propped against the side of the dresser. What has this child done? I excavate a pair of trousers from the pile and pull them on, then replace my socks and boots.

The girl will answer my questions or else... What will I do? Harm her?

Never again. Not intentionally.

I hadn't meant to harm Cordelia, and yet I had. My vow means nothing since I have no control over the beast within.

I approach the girl, standing close enough I could kiss her if I wanted. Yes, I want to do that—and more. But I will never touch this creature. "Where did you get the medallion?"

"From here. This town. Some old guy cornered me in an alley and gave me that thing."

"Speak sense, or I will—" Issue more empty threats. She doesn't need to know I will never hurt her, not intentionally.

"You'll do what?" she asks in a snide tone.

I grind my teeth and fist my hands.

"That's what I thought," she says with no small measure of sarcasm. "I need to pee, and I don't know how to use a chamber pot."

"You squat and urinate, that's how."

"I am not doing that in front of you."

"As you wish." I give her the chamber pot and turn my back. "Do it quickly."

Silence ensues for several seconds, then I hear her making use of the pot. "I'm done, *Sheriff.*"

Grabbing the pot, I throw open a window and dump the contents into the area just behind the outhouse.

I march back to her. "If you need to relieve yourself later, you may empty the chamber pot as I did."

"Ew. That's not sanitary."

"Nevertheless, it is your only option."

The girl puckers her lips and tips her head to the side. "You don't sound like Colin Firth."

"Is he your lover? Or your betrothed?" My breathing has become quicker, shallower, and I feel the need to batter this Colin Firth she mentioned.

She rolls her eyes. "Oh please. Colin Firth is an actor. He starred in the best version of *Pride & Prejudice.* But he sounds like an earl or whatever. You don't."

I suppose she means I don't speak in accordance with her preconceived ideas about members of the peerage. Though I've heard of Jane Austen's novel *Pride & Prejudice*, I have never read it. No man would deign to peruse a story full of romantic rubbish. Did someone produce a stage version of it? I've not heard of such a thing, but then, I was hardly welcome at society gatherings.

"Please forgive me," I say with acid in my tone. "I failed to live up to your expectations of an earl. Perhaps you would rather I toss you out on the street where I found you and let the locals have their fun."

"Where are you from?"

"England." Does she suffer from amnesia?

"I meant where in England."

"No more questions." My attention wanders to her chest, where her dressing gown has fallen open just enough to give me a tantalizing glimpse of her breasts. My breathing grows harsher and faster.

She holds the lapels of her dressing gown closed with one hand. "I need those clothes you promised me."

Yes, she does. Her lack of substantial clothing is eroding my willpower. The beast within craves her flesh. That creamy, soft, warm flesh.

"I told you that Lucy will find you appropriate garments to wear," I all but growl. "She should be here any moment."

And I should leave. But I can't convince my body to obey my commands and leave this room. I stand here like a marble statue.

Her lips are pink and full—and, I imagine, soft and supple. Against my wishes, my gaze wanders down her body, over the gentle curve of her belly and past her hips, stalling at her thighs. My mind torments me with a fantasy of grasping those hips while I fuck her from behind and she's on her hands and knees in front of me.

I growl deep in my throat.

The girl's eyes widen a touch, and she clutches her dressing gown more tightly. Her fear lasts only for the briefest moment, then she glares at me. "Remember what I said, Lord Nutjob. If you try to rape me—"

"Lord what?"

"Nutjob." She sighs and rolls her eyes. "Guess you Victorian people don't have that word yet. It means you're deranged. And a jerk. Very rude too."

"I've lived in America for five years, but I have never heard anyone use that term. Which means it is not only 'Victorian people,' as you call us, who have no knowledge of that word."

"Whatever."

Before I can ask what I'm meant to glean from that single word, without any context whatsoever, the door swings open. I'd left it unlocked, knowing Lucy would arrive soon with appropriate garments for this...irritating woman.

Lucy is carrying a bundle of clothing in her arms, wadded up so I can't tell what precisely she has chosen for the strange woman who now occupies my bedroom. Lucy stops near the girl and jerks her head toward the door. "Scram, Lord Wolfie. Ain't proper for a gentleman such as you to be in the room when his lady friend's gettin' gussied up for him."

Naturally, her voice drips with sarcasm.

"I will be outside the door," I tell Lucy with a slight snarl in my voice. "And make haste, woman. I'm certain my guest is getting cold."

Her stiff nipples jut against the slippery fabric of her dressing gown and the flimsy garment she wears underneath it, so yes, I am certain she feels a chill. She can't be...aroused.

I flee the room, pulling the door shut behind me. And I wait.

Leaning against the wall beside the door, I resist the fantasies that assail me once again when I think about what garments Lucy might have chosen for the woman who has become my charge. I can't very well allow her to roam free in this lawless, godless town. How did she come upon this place? Last night, I had assumed she wandered into the Outlands on her own after escaping from an asylum. But I know that is not the case. No one stumbles onto this town. No one escapes from it either.

The question remains. How and why did she come to be here?

"Why" seems obvious. She's here to further my torment, to ensure I suffer for my sins.

I lean to the side, laying my cheek against the cold metal of the door, and press my ear to it. Though I can hear voices, I can't understand the words they speak.

The door is wrenched open.

I stumble into Lucy, who flashes me a scowl.

"Back off, Yer Lordyship," she says. "If ya mean to have your way with that girl, at least do it on the floor. Easier to clean up the mess once you're done gnawin' on her."

She knows bloody well I have never viciously defiled a woman—not here in the Outlands. Lucy can't know of anything from my past. She wants to annoy me, and she succeeds.

"Return to the bar," I snarl at her. "And mind your own business for once. You know what I can do to you if I choose."

Lucy's eyes widen briefly, and I know she understands my meaning. She scurries down the hall, heading for the stairs.

I return to the bedroom and slam the door.

All the blood vacates my upper body, flooding into my loins.

The woman—Kylie stands there wearing a scarlet dress that features a fleur-de-lis pattern etched into the satin fabric and two layers of ruffles along the hem. The bodice clings to her torso, accentuating her breasts, and only two narrow straps secure the garment. The neckline reveals a hint of the luscious mounds of her breasts, and it's trimmed in black lace. Three lines of black piping curve down her chest to her waist, inexorably drawing my attention to the juncture of her thighs. I can't see her thighs, but I can see the black fishnet stockings that cling to her legs.

Does she wear garters underneath that dress?

My mind conjures an image of Kylie lifting her skirt for me, so I can duck my head beneath it and remove her garters with my teeth.

I clench my fists, but I can't stop my gaze from traveling down her calves. Black boots with two-inch heels cover her feet and ankles, their laces snugly tied. I clench my jaw too, and I can't stop a soft growl from escaping my lips.

She plants her hands on her hips. "What's wrong with you now? I'm wearing clothes, as you commanded." She lifts her skirt just enough to reveal her knee, glances down, then drops the fabric. "Isn't this a saloon-girl outfit? I don't work for you."

Lucy did this on purpose, didn't she? That woman finds enormous humor in vexing me, though I can cow her quite easily. I know she could've found an appropriate gown for Kylie to wear, but of course, she chose one designed to bring out the beast in me.

"I apologize for the clothing," I say. "Lucy has a bizarre sense of humor. The damnable woman thinks she owns this establishment. But she works for me, after a fashion. You do not."

Kylie stares at me without blinking. "You apologize?"

"Yes." Since I have no idea how long I'll be forced to have this woman under my aegis, I must stop snarling and growling at her. Mustn't I? It's been far too long since I needed to worry about the proper way of doing...anything.

"Am I still your hostage?" she asks.

"When I am in the building, you may leave this room—but only to go downstairs and only if I am present. For the remainder of the time, when I'm away, you must stay in this room for your own safety."

"So I am a prisoner, except when I have my jailer at my side."

"Yes." I move toward her without realizing I've done it until I'm standing an arm's length from her. "That dress is...becoming."

"Thanks, I guess. Not sure being complimented on looking like a Wild West hussy is something I should be grateful for, though."

Her lips curl up at the corners just enough to carve out dimples in her cheeks.

She's not angry anymore. Why? I am still behaving as her "jailer," or perhaps abductor is more accurate.

My gaze gravitates to her legs and those black stockings. My cock aches with a need I cannot, will not, ever satiate.

"Listen," she says, "there's something I need to tell you, though you'll probably think I'm crazy."

"I have lived through experiences far more insane than anything you could tell me."

She takes a deep breath, which hoists her breasts. "I think I kind of...time-traveled here."

"Time-traveled?"

"Yeah. I come from the twenty-first century. But last night, I had this freaky thing happen to me, and then—whoosh. I woke up in the Wild West with creepy cowboys leering at me."

"I don't understand."

"Neither do I. But trust me, I'm a twenty-first-century woman, not an eighteen-ninety-whatever saloon girl." She cocks her head. "What year is this, anyway?"

"Eighteen ninety-three." I can't decide whether she genuinely believes the nonsense she just told me or if she is insane after all.

"Wow. That's, like, a hundred and something years' difference." She laughs nervously, hunching her shoulders. "Sorry, I'm not great at doing math in my head."

She looks adorable and sweet when she laughs like that.

Kylie glances around, biting her bottom lip. "Um, why do you have a metal room that's got scratches on the floor and the wallpaper?"

My gaze veers to the floor between our feet and the deep gouges in it.

I clear my throat. "Are you hungry? I can bring your meal to you in here, or you could accompany me down to the saloon."

"Wow, you're going to let me out of my cage. Sure, I'd like that." She smiles in a way that seems almost playful. "Maybe you aren't a total nutjob after all, Mr. I'm Not Colin Firth."

"You would do well never to mention your favorite actor in my presence again." Because the beast within is rousing and growing jealous of that bastard. I do not want to feel envy. I do not want to feel anything for this woman. But my body cares nothing for my wishes and forces me to endure a lust that grows deeper and more ravenous with every passing moment that I remain in her presence.

Kylie rolls her eyes. "Jeez, you're uptight."

I take one step toward her, narrowing the space between us to a few inches. "You would also do well to stop harassing me. Every time you provoke my ire, I experience a growing need to possess you in every way imaginable, if only to make you cease talking."

My voice has grown deeper and rougher, so that I'm almost growling those words. The need to claim her body intensifies every time I'm in the same room with her.

She stares at me again, without blinking as before, but her pupils have enlarged and her breathing has grown labored. The sight of her breasts rising and falling drives me mad, but when she rakes her tongue across her bottom lip, I must summon all my willpower to stop myself from throwing her down on the bed and defiling that beautiful body.

Her gaze lands on my mouth, and she licks her bottom lip again.

Bloody hell. Now I'm breathing harder too.

Kylie glances down at the bulge of my hard cock and catches her bottom lip between her teeth, releasing it slowly while she keeps staring at my loins.

"Stop that," I growl.

Her gaze flicks up to mine. Her eyes are glossy, and her lips have turned a deeper shade of pink. "What?"

"I said stop that. Do not stare at my cock, please."

"Well, at least you said please." She smiles in the soft way she had a moment ago, and those dimples form in her cheeks again. "You know, you're not half bad when you aren't snarling at me. In fact, you're kind of hot."

Perhaps I do feel hot from the lust boiling inside me, but I have no idea how she can detect that.

She leans closer, though I don't think she does it intentionally. Her gaze connects with mine, and her lips part, begging me to devour them—to devour her.

"You think you want me to kiss you," I say. "But you have no conception of what I could do to you. I am not a gentleman. I am, quite literally, a beast."

"I'm not afraid of you. Maybe I should be, but I'm not."

My body seems to have a will of its own, urging me to inch closer until she must bend her head back to look at me. The movement exposes her throat, and I can see the pulse throbbing there as blood courses through the artery. I could rip her throat open and gorge on that blood. Part of me craves the taste of it, metallic and sweet. What I most want to experience, though, is the flavor of her desire.

The beast within has come fully awake, demanding I unleash it.

Not yet. Daylight is my time, not yours.

I duck my head to her throat, sniffing to draw in her scent. I smell fear, yes, though not much. She hadn't lied when she told me she is not afraid of me. Beneath the faint aroma of fear, I detect other things I can't describe. Sweet. Heady. Arousing. I could feast on her for days and never get enough. Why must she smell like everything I've hungered for the most? Every time I inhale through my nostrils, the aroma of her sinks deeper inside me.

"Are you seriously sniffing me?" she asks, her voice rife with breathless desire.

"Yes. I'm capturing a sample of your scent, and it's intoxicating."

"Oh, um, that's...weird." She has begun to breathe heavily as if overcome by the desire mounting inside her.

The scent of her is driving me mad.

I grasp her shoulders and drag her into me, possessing her mouth, crushing my lips to hers, enveloped by the aroma of her need and drowned in the sensation of her skin touching mine.

She moans so softly I almost don't hear it, and I smell her growing lust. She wants me, and heaven help me, I want her. More than want her. I hunger for this woman like I have never hungered for anything in my life. To plunge inside her body and possess her in every way... I need it too much.

I should pull away, but I can't.

CHAPTER SIX

Kylie

NATHANIEL IS KISSING ME. HIS LIPS FEEL WARM AS THEY PRESS INTO mine with more and more strength, like he wants to consume me completely. But he doesn't. I relax my jaw, waiting for him to push his tongue inside my mouth, but he doesn't do that either. Still, I can't stop myself from sagging into him and moaning again, louder this time, with a desperate need he seems determined not to quench.

I'm about to take the lead and thrust my tongue between his lips, but I don't get the chance.

He jerks away from me, staggering backward a few steps, and gapes at me like he's never seen me before.

I feel so warm and liquid, like I might melt into a puddle at his feet and love it. Maybe he'll lap me up and—

Nathaniel pivots on his heels, stalks to the door, and rips it open.

The woman who brought me the dress I'm wearing is hovering outside the door with her head turned to the side. She seems to be exactly where the door was a second ago.

Was she eavesdropping? I think she might've been.

Nathaniel shoves her backward and slams the door behind them both.

I consider my options for about half a second, then march to the door and plaster my ear to it.

"What are you playing at?" he demands in that sexy, growly tone I've heard often. This time, he sounds angry, not lustful. "Never listen at my door again. Do you understand me?"

"I was only making sure ya didn't need nothing. Sure don't need her, not when ya got me, lover."

"We are not lovers."

"But I can give you—"

Foot scuffling. A grunt. A gasp.

"Do you have any idea," he snarls, "how easily I could snap your neck?"

"Sorry," she mumbles, her voice unsteady.

"Obey me or suffer the consequences."

"Yeah, sure, whatever you say."

"And bring food for the girl. *Now.*"

Footsteps recede, but only one pair of them as far as I can tell.

The doorknob rotates.

I scuttle backward until my thighs meet the bed.

Nathaniel hurls the door open and stomps up to me. "You will remain here. With me. Lucy will fetch us food, which we will eat together, in this room."

His hair is messy, and a few locks have fallen over his forehead. Disheveled looks surprisingly good on him, as does his shadow beard, but I could do without the angry expression on his face.

My heart is pounding. Had I lied when I said I wasn't afraid of him? No, I hadn't. But I suddenly realize this isn't fear coursing through my veins. A wave of heat sweeps over me from head to toe and sets off a liquid tingle between my thighs. What is wrong with me? I want this man who abducted me and locked me up in a pretty little cave above a saloon. The man who growls at me. The hottest British cowboy I've ever seen.

Yeah, I've lost my mind.

I can't think of what to say to him, and my brain is not helping me at all. My libido seems to have taken control. So naturally, I say something dumb. "Chill out, hey?"

His brows squish together, and he tips his head to the side. "What variety of female creature are you?"

Variety? Creature? Okay, I might take back that stuff I thought about how hot he is. On second thought, no. He might be nutty and a smidge dangerous, but in the last few minutes, I've discovered I like bad boys who are also wickedly hot British cowboy sheriffs. I'd loved that kiss. No one has ever kissed me the way Nathaniel Fortescue did, and I'd burned for him to go deeper. Christ, I'd all but begged him to do that with my body language and my moaning. He'd told me he's literally a beast, and though I have no clue what that means, hearing him speak those words made me want to jump him.

So yeah, I'm nuts too. We're quite a pair.

Does he mean "beast" as in wild animal? The man does growl like one. I'd wondered about that last night, but no, it's impossible. He can't be an animal, except in the sense of being a man. Humans are animals, after all.

But he growls like a...wolf.

My gaze shifts to the floor and the deep claw marks there. What kind of beast did that?

"I am not a creature," I say, looking him straight in the eye. Well, sort of askew in the eye since he's still got his head tipped sideways. "I'm a woman, an American, and an ornithology student."

His head jerks upright, and his brows lift. "You study birds?"

Does he have to sound shocked by that fact? "That's right, Mr. I'm a Literal Beast. The child-creature you're holding prisoner isn't a dummy after all. I'm working on my master's, for your information. When I got my bachelor's degree, I graduated summa cum laude."

Nathaniel stares at me for several seconds, his face blank.

The silence becomes deafening and awkward, so I opt to fill it with inane things. "Does anyone call you Nate?"

"No."

"How about Nat?"

"No."

I wrap my arms around myself because this room is kind of drafty and this dress has no sleeves. "Don't you have a nickname at all? I mean, my name is too short for that, but yours—"

He clomps up to me, halting so close that, once again, I need to tilt my head back to see his face.

Damn, he's tall. And muscular. And he smells oddly good, like the outdoors and spices.

Bending his head, he gazes into my eyes. "No one who wishes to continue breathing ever calls me anything but Sheriff Nathaniel Fortescue."

"That's a mouthful to say every time I need to get your attention."

"Call me Sheriff, then."

"Oh come on, that's not a very friendly name. We kissed, in case you've forgotten." I push up onto my tiptoes, and our lips brush against each other for a split second. That was an accident, I swear. "You can call me Kylie."

"If you insist." His voice has gotten rougher again like it had right before he kissed me. "I suppose you might as well call me Nathaniel."

"Thank you."

"But you will never refer to me as Nate or Nat."

"Ten-four, Sheriff."

His entire face squishes up this time.

"Sorry," I say. *Duh, Kylie, they don't have trucker slang in the Wild West.* "Sometimes I forget this isn't the twenty-first century or even the twentieth. Ten-four means I understand."

He is pretty darn cute when he's flummoxed.

Nathaniel takes two steps back.

I sit down on the bed's edge. "May I ask a nosy question?"

He sighs, then waves his hand in a go-on gesture. "If you must."

"Thank you." I study him for a second, then ask away. "What is a British earl doing in a dingy old frontier town? And how did you become sheriff?"

And are you sleeping with Lucy? I want to know, but I shouldn't ask that. I shouldn't care, anyway. He told her they're not lovers, but the present tense suggests they could've been once.

He takes his leather coat off and tosses it onto the headboard, where it dangles from a post. Then he drags a chair out of the corner and sets it down beside the bed, at the opposite end from where I'm sitting. He props his boot-clad feet on the mattress. "What am I doing here? Serving my penance, and that's all the answer you will receive. How did I become sheriff? No one else wanted the job after my predecessor was viciously murdered."

"Are you serious? He was murdered?"

"Yes. Torn to shreds might be a more apt description."

I swallow. Hard. Torn to shreds? I can't help wondering if he did the shredding since he claims to be a literal beast. But no, I can't believe that. Why, I haven't got a clue. Somehow, deep down where my intuition lies, I know he would never intentionally hurt someone unless they gave him no choice.

Still, I have to ask. "Did, um, you kill the sheriff?"

"No. The Outlands houses every variety of miscreant and deviant known to mankind. One of them killed my predecessor."

"Why would you want to be sheriff after that? Don't you worry about being the next man who gets filleted?"

He nails his gaze to mine, and a hot shiver ripples through me. "No one would dare challenge me."

"Lucy does."

"An impudent whore is no threat to me."

"I, uh, challenge you too. Don't I?"

He narrows his eyes. "Perhaps you do, but I have ways to tame you if necessary."

"Please," I huff. "Nobody tames me. I'm a liberated woman."

Maybe I did get a teeny bit tingly when he announced he could tame me, but I will never tell him so.

I scoot closer to him, stopping near his feet. "What kind of beast are you?"

"What I am is of no consequence to you."

"Since I'm your prisoner, I think it is of consequence to me."

A knock at the door interrupts our bizarre conversation.

"Got the chow," Lucy hollers. "Ya gonna unlock the door, Lord Wolfie?"

"It *is* unlocked," Nathaniel shouts.

The door pivots inward, and Lucy carries a tray of food into the room, halting halfway to us. Her gaze darts from Nathaniel to me several times before settling on him. "Where you want me to put the chow?"

"Bring the tray to me."

The sharpness of his tone makes Lucy cringe for a second. She complies with his order but keeps glancing sideways at me.

Nathaniel scowls at her. "You are dismissed."

She scuttles out of the room, shutting the door.

"Why does she call you Lord Wolfie?" I ask.

"Because she is an insolent female."

That's all I get out of him, so we eat in silence. The food is passable, and I'm not too picky this morning since I haven't eaten in so long I can't remember when that was. Once we finish our meal, Nathaniel grabs the tray and his coat and heads for the door.

"Are you locking me in again?"

He pauses with his hand on the doorknob. After a few seconds, he sighs. "No, I am not locking you in."

Nathaniel turns around and tosses me his key.

I catch it. "What are you doing?"

"You will lock yourself inside this room. Do not leave. This is for your own protection." He sharpens his gaze on me. "Will you do as I say?"

"No promises. I don't like to lie, and I'm not sure I can trust you, so I can't promise not to leave this room. I'll take your wishes into consideration. That's the best I can do."

He stares at me for a moment, then walks out the door, slamming it shut.

I get up and lock myself in. Well, at least this time I have the key. I also have the medallion, which I retrieve from his ruined pants and hide under the mattress for safekeeping.

A medallion with a wolf on it. Last night, I heard howling. That's what drew me away from the hotel and back to the ghost town. I dreamed of a wolf howling while I slept in this room, but I also felt like I'd woken up briefly and heard that sound for real.

Nathaniel growls. He calls himself a beast. He lives in a room that has claw-like gouges in the floor and is encased in metal. Lucy calls him Lord Wolfie.

Oh no, I am not even considering the idea. Well, time travel is real. Why not... No way. But I've watched enough horror movies and read enough novels to recognize the signs. Those are fiction, though. Modern myths. Nathaniel Fortescue cannot be a werewolf.

Even thinking the word makes me feel foolish and kind of ooky.

I'll think about that stuff later.

Nathaniel asked me to stay in this room, so I decide to oblige him. Why am I doing what he asked? Because I'm not stupid. Even I sense there's something eerie about this town and the people in it—especially Nathaniel Fortescue.

CHAPTER SEVEN

Nathaniel

I STAND OUTSIDE THE DOOR FOR SEVERAL MINUTES, NOT MOVING, SIMply listening and sniffing the air. Christ, even with a metal barrier between us, I can still smell her. I hear her too, moving about in the room, restless and no doubt annoyed with me for ordering her to remain in there alone. I should have returned her from whence she came, but I have no idea where that is.

Or when, if I believe her claim. Traveling through time? It sounds ridiculous.

Then again, I am not a normal man. This town is not normal either, and the residents confined here certainly do not qualify as average humans. Perhaps I ought not dismiss Kylie's claim out of hand.

I drag myself away from the door and make my way downstairs. Men, if the males in this town can be called men, are talking and laughing, drinking and making lewd comments to the women who work here. Saloon girls know how to handle these blackguards, and I will only intervene if and when it becomes necessary.

When I step off the last stair, the saloon falls silent. Every gaze veers to me.

Lucy rushes out from behind the bar, reaching for the tray I'm carrying. "Lemme take that, Lord Wolf—Sheriff Fortescue."

Yes, she's always far more courteous after I've chastised her.

"Thank you," I say crisply as I shrug into my coat. "If I have not returned by midday, please ensure my guest receives a meal."

Lucy braces the tray against her hip. "Ain't got the key, Sheriff, beggin' your pardon."

"The girl has it. Knock and announce your intentions." Of course, I did command Kylie to keep herself locked in that room. And she told me she couldn't promise to obey me. *Damn and blast.* "Leave the meal at the door. She will retrieve it herself."

I gave her the key to my room, which means she can let herself out if she wishes. Considering how much she relishes defying me, I should expect her to attempt to flee. If she does, it may be her last mistake.

I stride out of the saloon into the sallow light of the morning sun and swerve left to head for the sheriff's office—my office. For the next several hours, I patrol my domain. Though I had told Kylie the Outlands belongs to me, that's not strictly true. For reasons I do not understand, I have taken it upon myself to ride herd on the degenerates and miscreants who occupy this town. Not everyone here harbors ill intent toward others, but all have committed some sort of transgression that consigned them to this place.

And yes, that includes me.

The worst offense I witness this morning is a drunkard who has vomited on the steps of the general store. I lock the man in a cell in the sheriff's office. The Outlands is rarely this quiet, and the peaceful nature of the day so far leaves me with a prickling sense of unease deep under my skin. Why should the deviants under my aegis suddenly become peaceful? What has changed? The only difference between yesterday and today is...

She came.

I wander back to the saloon and upstairs to the doorway behind which she hides. No one speaks as I cross the saloon floor, though everyone stares at me. Just as I approach the bedroom door, it swings open.

Kylie hovers there, bent at the waist, her attention focused on the tray of food sitting a few inches past the threshold. She reaches for the tray.

I step up to it.

She startles, letting out a half-suppressed cry.

From this angle, I can see down the neckline of her dress where the creamy slopes of her breasts are visible. My groin tightens.

"Get up," I say, my voice rough with a need only she provokes in me. I cannot succumb, no matter how badly I want to do it.

Kylie puckers her lips, slowly rising from her crouch.

"Take the food," I hiss.

She manages to both flatten her lips and keep them puckered, then she picks up the tray. "Whatever you command, Your Highness."

I stride forward, forcing her to back into the room, and shut the door behind me. "Your Highness is not the proper form of address for an earl."

"Thought you weren't an earl anymore. You're the sheriff of a creepy-ass town."

Creepy-ass? I understand no more than one-fifth of what she says.

"What language do you speak?" I ask. "You claim to be American, but I've not heard anyone in this country speak the way you do."

"That's because I speak twenty-first-century American." She sets the tray down on the bedside table and eyes me with her gaze narrowed and her mouth twisted to one side. "You probably don't know modern British either, huh? Love the coat, by the way. It's wicked cool."

"Perhaps you could try to speak a version of the English language that does not involve...whatever colloquialisms you have been employing."

"How long have you lived in this town? Earlier, you said you've been in America for five years."

"Yes, and I've spent four and a half years in the Outlands." I've no idea why I'm answering her question. But I allow myself the brief pleasure of drinking in the vision of her in that dress. "How old are you?"

"Rude much? A real gentleman doesn't ask a question like that."

"As I have told you, I am not a gentleman. I never was." I take three steps toward her. "How old are you?"

"Twenty-four. I'm only telling you because I feel like it, not because you demanded to know, you big hairy beast."

She has no idea how accurate that description is.

One more time, I rake my gaze over her luscious body. "Are you married or betrothed?"

"No."

"Are you being courted?"

She rolls her eyes. "Yeah, I've got every man in this creepy-ass town begging to 'court' me. What do you think? No, I don't have a boyfriend. Why am I telling you anything? Unless you share something about yourself, I won't be answering your nosy questions anymore."

"As you wish. Ask, and I will answer."

She folds her arms over her chest. "How did you wind up here? In this country, in this town, as the sheriff."

For a moment, I consider refusing to answer—or lying to her. But I don't want to do either of those. I haven't the slightest notion of why, but I want to tell her the truth. One small part of it. "No member of the peerage ever accepted me, but the events that transpired shortly before my departure..." I rub my jaw, avoiding her gaze. "Catastrophic might be the most accurate term for it."

I feel her watching, feel her curiosity burning into me.

"What is the peerage?" she asks. "You said it means you're titled, but I'm still confused."

"The term peerage refers to peers of the realm, which means anyone who holds a title they inherited or that was bestowed on them by the queen. Duke, earl, et cetera."

"So did you inherit your title?"

"Ostensibly."

Kylie huffs a breath out through her nostrils. "What is that supposed to mean?"

"Enough questions." I lean toward her. "Unless you would care to tell me all your secrets."

"You suck at conversation. And at being a decent human being." She stabs a finger into my chest. "Actually, you just suck, period. Don't care how hot you are."

"I am not feeling warm at the moment, but if you persist in making movements that jostle your bosom, I may become hotter than you would ever wish me to be."

She squints at me. "I don't think you're using the word hot in the same way I am."

"Yes, I agree. I speak the Queen's English, and you speak...a barbarian tongue."

"Barbarian?" she says with a laugh. "Wow, you really are uptight. How far is that stick wedged up your ass?"

"My arse does not have sticks in it." I grasp her shoulders. "No more talking, unless you want me to ravage you."

She angles toward me, her breasts rising and falling with each breath. "What if I do want that? I bet you don't have the balls to follow through."

I would tear the heart from my chest if that would stop her from speaking in a sultry voice. She's rousing the beast within and has no conception of what doing so will wreak on her.

"Must you vex me?" I snarl.

"Yes, I must. You need serious vexing, Lord Anal Retentive."

I growl softly, struggling to keep hold of the beast's reins. "Eat your meal and trouble me no further."

Summoning every iota of willpower within in me, I trudge toward the door. My feet refuse to move any faster. My body wants me to seize the girl and have my way with her, damn the consequences. But I force my feet to move, my boots scraping across the wood floor.

Kylie rushes past me to the door. She shoves the key into her bodice.

I halt halfway to her, breathing hard, every exhalation infused with a low growl. "What are you doing, you foolish child?"

"Don't stuffy Victorian Brits think twenty-four is over the hill? For a woman, I mean."

There is a faint note of fear in her voice. Or is that excitement? I lift my chin and sniff the air. Her desire tantalizes my senses and stirs the beast even more, and everything inside me, from my skin to my cock, comes alive with the searing need to claim her body.

Her breasts, heaving. Her lips, parted. Her eyes, darkening.

In the face of her lust, I can't control myself any longer. The last thread of restraint within me snaps.

And I leap on her, crushing her body to mine. The iron erection barely contained in my trousers presses into her belly, and all I can think of is how good it will feel to plunge into her body.

She gazes up at me, her lips curving into the barest of smiles. "Nathaniel, I—"

"Do not speak," I growl, the sound so deep and animalistic that I scarcely recognize my own voice. "I cannot—will not—relinquish you."

"I don't want you to let go. I'm not afraid of you."

"You stupid girl." I spin her around and lash my arms about her waist, pinning her arms at her sides. Though her breasts are no longer crushed to me, I now have a perfect view down her bodice. "You want me to fuck you. I can smell your desire, can almost taste it."

"Yes, I want that."

"If you knew what I could do to you—"

"Don't care."

"Kylie..." I slide a hand up her body, over those lush breasts, and higher to her neck. My fingers encircle her throat but remain slack. "I could break your neck with one hand."

"You won't. I know it."

I speak directly into her ear, my lips scraping her flesh. "You know nothing."

"Then show me."

"If you insist." I keep my fingers around her throat as I glide my other hand down, past her hips, and thrust it under her dress to push my fingers between her thighs. "I want to grasp your bodice and tear your dress to shreds with my bare hands, then throw you down on the bed and mount you like a wild beast. It won't be tender or careful. I will fuck you so hard you'll feel as if your body might shatter, but no matter how much you scream for me to stop, I won't be able to. I can't promise you will enjoy, much less survive, what I will do to you."

She has begun to breathe so hard that she's almost gasping. "Do it, Nathaniel. Do it now."

My cock throbs, and the beast clamors to be released. "You don't even know what I am."

"What if I do? I'm not as clueless as you think."

"I doubt you know as much as you believe you do."

She slides her tongue across her bottom lip. "You're a werewolf, aren't you?"

"What?" I remain utterly still, unable even to convince my mind to function. She can't know, and yet she does. How has this woman divined my secret? I have many more, but if she could deduce one, she might uncover them all. "Why would you suggest such a thing? No one on earth would reach that conclusion."

"I'm not like all you people. I come from the future, where we have books and movies and even songs about men who become wolves when the moon is full."

She knows enough to endanger herself, but not enough to realize what jeopardy she has placed herself in.

Though I have no idea how, I summon just enough of my tattered self-control to force myself to release her. Then I stagger backward.

Kylie turns toward me, still gasping, and slides her tongue across her bottom lip again.

Take her now, the beast howls in my mind.

I hurry out of the room, nearly knocking her over in my haste, and flee the saloon in search of somewhere I can hide from the woman who has uncaged the wolf within.

What if I can't hide from her?

Blood will spill, but it won't be the first time I've ravaged a woman.

CHAPTER EIGHT

Kylie

I STARE AT THE DOOR FOR A MINUTE OR TWO AFTER NATHANIEL BOLT-ed, bumping into me in the process. I need that long to catch my breath and recover from whatever it was that just happened between us. He felt me up, that's for sure. He growled and sniffed me like a dog—or a wolf. The jerk threatened to screw me, then ran away. I can't decide if I'm angry because he didn't do that or because he wanted to do it.

Maybe both.

Okay, yes, I have a bizarre and unhealthy attraction to him. It can't be good for me to want a man who's also a wild beast, a man who locks me up in his metal-encased bedroom and demands to know why I "vex" him. Well, dammit, he vexes me too. I don't care how hot he is or how amazingly he kisses. That man had better start showing me some respect or I'll follow through on my threat to make him bleed from his eyes and his dick.

Except I probably can't do that. He's too strong.

But there is something about him...

I whirl away from the door, my gaze flying to the spot under the mattress where I stashed the medallion earlier. Something tugs at me, something indescribable and inexplicable, and I find myself walking to the bed. I reach under the mattress to pull out the medallion. The shaman who gave it to me had seemed Native American and said his people "once lived" in the area surrounding the ghost town. But I'm not in that place anymore. I've traveled back in time to meet a British werewolf who lives in an eerie version of Wrathrock filled with sinister people.

Sheesh, how much weirder can my life get?

I'm not doubting my circumstances anymore. Is that a bad sign? Even if I'm lying in a mental hospital somewhere and hallucinating all of this, I might as well roll with it. But I know I'm not crazy. Which probably means I am.

Whatever.

Cupping the medallion in my left hand, I run my right index finger over the lines engraved on its surface. The five-pointed star reminds me of a sheriff's badge. Nathaniel's leather coat had a badge like that pinned to it. I'm pretty sure the image on the medallion is exactly like the sheriff's star on his coat. I turn the medallion over to examine the image of a wolf howling. Just like the first time I'd seen this metal disk, I get the impression the imagery isn't Native American. It reminds me of Old World Europe, though I can't explain why or in what way. It makes no sense for a Native American shaman to give me a European medallion.

When Nathaniel had grabbed the thing, right before his pants caught fire, he had seemed to recognize it.

That means I need to talk to the rude man again.

I glance down at my saloon hussy outfit. First, I need to get some real clothes.

Leaving the medallion in here seems like a bad idea, so I tuck it inside my bodice under my left boob. The bedroom key is under my right boob.

I let myself out and lock the door behind me. Sheriff Asshat probably doesn't want any nosy townsfolk snooping around in his little fortress. I head downstairs and ignore the men who shout come-ons and make catcalls. Lucy is manning the bar, so I pause there to get information.

"Where can I get some clothes?" I ask.

"General store." She puckers her lips as she gives me a visual once-over. "They ain't got girlie stuff, ya know. Won't find nothing you can wear."

I want to respond with a sarcastic comment, but I decide that's not the smartest move. "Thank you for the information, Lucy. I appreciate your advice. Where can I find the general store?"

"Turn right. You'll see it." She sneers at me. "Hard to miss since it's right next door."

"Okay. Thank you." Yeah, I'd love to smack that expression off her face, but I won't give her the satisfaction of annoying me.

Just as I'm walking out the swinging doors, she hollers, "He ain't for your kind, missy. A slip of a thing like you can't handle Lord Wolfie."

That's bullshit since I handled him just fine earlier. I "vex" him, but I think that's a good thing. That man needs a lot of vexing, in my opinion. Everyone in this town seems to be afraid of him, so I imagine he's gotten used to people kowtowing to him and cowering in his presence. Sure, they get snarky with him, but their fear is obvious beneath the surface rudeness.

Why am I not afraid of him?

I ponder that question while I amble down the street to the next building over and head inside the general store.

The man behind the counter pushes up his glasses and sort of smiles, though he seems reluctant to even look at me. "Can I help you, miss?"

He sounds reluctant too.

"I need some clothes," I say.

All around me, I see shelves and tables chock-full of goods, everything from flour, coffee, and candy to toiletries and "patent medicines," whatever those are. I also see bolts of cloth and equipment for sewing. Luckily, the store has ready-made clothing too.

I walk over to a table full of clothes, picking up a pair of wool pants and holding them to my body to see if they'd fit.

"What are you doing?" the store clerk asks as he rushes over to snatch the pants from me. "These are for men. We don't carry clothing for women, so you'll need to sew it yourself."

He points to a collection of sewing paraphernalia on a table nearby.

I have no idea how to sew a dress.

"Women can wear pants too, you know," I tell the man. "Calamity Jane does."

"Sure, but she's, uh, more like a man than..." He trails off and makes a pained face. "Can't I show you some nice cotton fabric instead?"

My information about Calamity Jane comes from the Doris Day movie about her. Guess I got it right despite using Hollywood as my historical source. The store clerk seems to think a woman who wears pants isn't a real woman. Nathaniel probably does too.

"What's your name?" I ask the clerk. "I'm Kylie Drummond."

I offer him my hand.

He stares at it for a moment, then shakes my hand like he's afraid I'm contagious. "Clay Garfield. I run the store for the sheriff."

"Nathaniel owns it?"

"Well, not as such. He's sort of in charge of the whole town, being sheriff and all." He glances at my bosom, what he can see of it thanks to this stupid dress, then veers his attention to my face and clears his throat. "You're, uh, the sheriff's girl. Aren't you?"

No, no, absolutely no. That's what I want to say, but claiming kinship with Nathaniel seems like the smarter choice. "Yes, I am. And he wants me to have whatever clothes I like."

Lying also seems like my best option right now. No way am I traipsing around in this creepy town while dressed like a floozy.

Clay frowns down at the men's clothes on the table. "You'll need boy's sizes, I think."

He helps me pick out wool pants, a cotton shirt, socks, and boots without complaining. I pass on underwear since all Clay has in stock are "bloomers," which are baggy pants-like things that won't fit under my pants. He does seem uncomfortable, but he doesn't try to talk me out of buying the clothes. And he puts it all on the sheriff's tab. I say that's the least Nathaniel can do for me after the way he's behaved.

I have a cowboy hat too.

Clay lets me go into his backroom to change. When I come out, I toss the saloon-girl outfit onto the counter. "Could you return these to Lucy for me?"

"Sure thing, miss."

"Thank you for your help, Clay. Do you know where the sheriff might be?"

"Sorry, miss, no. He does what he wants when he wants."

No shit.

I exit the store and step out onto the street. The medallion is in my left pocket now, though I don't think anyone will notice it's there. I left my shirt untucked, so it covers my hips. The room key is in my right pocket.

Where is Nathaniel? I need to have a serious talk with that man.

The medallion grows warm in my pocket.

I dig it out and hold it in my palm. The warmth dissipates, but I have the oddest feeling that the medallion wants to tell me something. Sure, because inanimate objects talk. I guess a girl who time-traveled shouldn't be so dismissive of weird things. Grasping the medallion's cord, I let the thing dangle from my fingers. The metal disk sways a little, its motion growing stronger instead of lessening, until it starts to rock back and forth.

Then the disk spins once and stops.

I squint at it. If this thing is trying to direct me, I have no idea how to interpret its movements. The wolf face is pointing down the street directly behind me. Should I go that way? Or am I supposed to choose the opposite direction, which is where the star face points?

The shaman had called me the "keeper of the wolf's destiny."

Not that I'm believing in that crap, but what the hell. I head in the direction the wolf's head on the medallion pointed me toward and stuff the thing back in my pocket. I pass by the saloon and some other buildings including a barbershop and a lawyer's office. I see the sheriff's office too, and though I pop in there, I don't find Nathaniel. A scruffy man is locked in a cell, but he's snoring and doesn't notice me. I go back outside and keep walking down the street.

It just kind of...ends. Desert unfurls away from me, broken only by a path worn down by horses, I imagine. It's too wide for deer but too narrow for wagons.

Yeah, I'm suddenly an expert on nineteenth-century transportation.

I swivel my head left, seeing nothing, and then right. That's when I see him, a shadow within the shadow of the last building.

Nathaniel leans against the structure, arms folded over his chest. His head is tipped down, his hat too, so I can't see his face.

A tingle rushes over my skin.

I am not excited to see him again. No way. But I do walk over to him and stop beside where he's leaning against the building. "Taking a nap? I thought sheriffs had, you know, sheriffing to do."

He lifts his head to glance at me. "Must you invent words? The English language is full enough as it is."

"I like inventing words. It's fun."

Nathaniel roves his gaze over my body, and his brows lift when he looks at my face again. "What are you wearing?"

"A kooky thing called clothes."

He opens his mouth—to complain about my wording, no doubt.

"I did not make up the word kooky," I say before he can speak. "It's legitimate. But I guess you old-timey people don't have that term yet."

"Perhaps you could teach me your language."

I stare at him. Even my eyelids can't seem to believe what he said, since they've stopped blinking. Did Sheriff Asshat just ask me to teach him something? Was he being nice? No, that can't be.

"You're being sarcastic," I say. "Every kooky thing I say makes you angry."

"No, it does not." He slings an arm around me and pulls my body against him. "It makes me want to kiss you."

CHAPTER NINE

Nathaniel

I DON'T *WANT* TO KISS HER. I *NEED* TO KISS HER. PERHAPS I CAN BLAME the wolf within, but I suspect this need has little to do with my inner beast. I find Kylie...enticing. Intoxicating. Refreshing. And other things I dare not think, much less speak aloud. I should snarl at her to go away. Instead, I told her I want to kiss her.

Never have I needed to taste a woman's lips as much as I need to taste hers. But I hunger for more than that. I crave her body, every inch of it, from her slender throat to her lush breasts, and lower still to the juncture of her thighs where the sweetest cream awaits. But I cannot touch her. Yes, I know I've done that already. Never again.

Why, then, do I have my arm lashed around her?

The feminine scent of her teases my senses, and I can't stop myself from inhaling a deep breath through my nostrils to revel in the aroma of her.

I do like every nonsensical word she speaks. I should not enjoy it, but I do. I like her clothing too. Wool trousers look sensual when she wears them, and her shirt that hangs loose makes me imagine all those curves I know hide beneath the fabric. She left two buttons unhooked on the shirt, which inexorably draws my focus toward her breasts. I can't see them, but I know they hide just below the spot where the third button lies hooked.

To devour her... It might be the most satisfying experience of my life.

But it will certainly become the worst nightmare she has ever endured—if she can endure it.

I shove her away. "Go back to the saloon and lock yourself in my room."

"No."

Why must she always harass me? I growl, hoping that might convince her I will brook no insolence. "Do as I say or—"

"Or what? You'll growl again? Or maybe this time you'll turn into a wolf right in front of me." She waves a hand. "Go on, do it. I dare you."

She truly is the most vexing creature I've ever met. "Whatever you believe you know about me and my true nature, witnessing it firsthand will prove you are wrong. But the knowledge will come too late, for you will already be dead."

"If I'm already dead, how can I realize I was wrong?"

A long, frustrated shout erupts out of me, and I shove myself away from the wall to round on Kylie. "Be silent. For once, do as I say."

"Why should I? You've given me zero reasons to follow your orders, Sheriff Asshat."

Sheriff what? I was correct when I wondered if she might belong in an asylum. I shouldn't ask for clarification, but I seem incapable of stopping myself. "My name is Nathaniel Fortescue, not Asshat. Is that a bizarre surname invented by Americans of your time?"

"It's not a name. It's an apt description." She twirls a finger in the air in the direction of my head. "You are a total ass, so you might as well wear it like a hat on your head. Understand now?"

No, not entirely. But I think I'm beginning to grasp the meaning of what she called me. She claims to dislike me because I am an arse of the greatest magnitude. Or something to that effect. And yet this morning she begged me to take her.

If I want her cooperation, perhaps I should try to growl less and limit the number of times per day that I command her to do my will. When I consider how often I've behaved like a ravenous wolf in her presence, I suffer an inexplicable impulse, one I can't ignore. So I rub my jaw, avoiding her gaze. "I apologize for my behavior toward you. It was inexcusable."

Kylie eyes me with what seems like a mixture of curiosity and annoyance. "Thank you, Nathaniel. I accept your apology. Maybe we could be friends if you'd stop growling at me."

She does not sound irritated anymore.

"Even if I wish to stop growling," I tell her, "I can't control it. The wolf exerts a powerful hold over me."

"You snarl at everybody all the time? No wonder the people in this creepy town seem like they're afraid of you and ticked at you at the same time."

"They despise me as much as I despise them. However, their fear of what I am, what I might do to them, outweighs their revulsion."

"Is that a long-winded way of saying you scare the shit out of them?"

"Yes, I suppose so. Though I assume you mean that as a metaphor. I have not frightened anyone to the point of incontinence."

One side of her mouth slants upward. "You don't scare me, Mr. I'm-A-Beast."

I know that, but her lack of fear makes no sense.

Kylie lodges her hands in the pockets of her trousers. "Here's a radical idea. Let's get to know each other. You know, have a conversation."

"Concerning what?"

She rolls her eyes. "You. Duh. I've got questions."

"Will I be afforded the opportunity to question you as well?"

"Yeah, sure. But you probably won't believe anything I tell you." She leans toward me, so close I can smell her. "Unless you've suddenly accepted that I'm from the future."

"I haven't the luxury of disbelief. I am a wolf, after all."

She tips her head to the side as if studying me. "How long have you been a werewolf?"

A tingle of awareness dances down my spine, but it's not desire for her. My senses, heightened by the wolf within, alert me to someone watching. Perhaps more than one someone.

"Not here," I tell Kylie. "We must go elsewhere, beyond the reach of spying eyes and ears. I know a place."

"Okay." She straightens and salutes me. "Lead the way, Sheriff."

"No one salutes a sheriff. That's strictly for the military."

"Whatever. Just take me to your secret hideaway."

"Don't you want to argue and roll your eyes?"

"Nope."

I study her for a moment, attempting to gauge her sincerity, but I neither see nor smell anything that suggests she's lying. This woman genuinely wants to accompany me to my "secret place" without having any idea where I might take her.

"Follow me," I say as I walk toward the street.

Kylie stays in step with me even when we head out into the desert where the only tracks are those of animals. The Outlands has no stagecoach route, no wagon trail, nothing that a civilized western town would have. I veer across the desert toward a butte not far from town, and Kylie keeps pace with me—without uttering a single complaint or sarcastic comment.

The butte rises perhaps one hundred feet above the desert floor with a diameter of several hundred feet. Its sides are steep, but the summit, once a sheer vertical drop, has collapsed into a rounded heap. We are not climbing the butte, though. I lead Kylie toward a spot on the western side of the formation at ground level. As we draw closer to it, the tension within me lessens a bit.

The butte itself conceals the entrance, hidden behind a section of rock that juts out from the main mass. Only within close proximity to the butte can anyone see the opening. No one comes here, though. No one other than me.

I pause at the entrance and offer my hand to Kylie. "This is it. Will you come inside with me?"

She slips her hand into mine. "Yes."

Perhaps I had expected her to balk at the idea of accompanying me into a darkened cave hidden behind a rock wall. And perhaps I'm stunned that she wants to come with me, anywhere.

I lead her into the darkness.

We travel a distance I know well—fifty feet, precisely, as I've measured it with my foot paces—until we emerge from the narrow entry passage into a larger chamber. It's too dark in here for Kylie to see, yet she follows me with her hand clasping mine. I smell no fear from her.

I halt us just inside the chamber. "I'll need to release your hand for a moment so I can light the lantern."

"All right." She lets go of my hand. "Hurry it up, though. I don't do well in dark, enclosed spaces."

I find the oil lantern I'd left in here and light it with a match from the box I'd also left inside the chamber.

Flickering light illuminates the cavern and burnishes Kylie's skin as if she has become a bronze statue of a Classical goddess, though deities never dressed in wool trousers as far as I know.

She squints for a moment, clearly adjusting to the change in lighting, from sunlight to darkness to lamplight. "Can you see in the dark?"

"I am a wolf, so yes, I can see in the dark."

"Cool."

"You're cold?" I remove my coat, offering it to her. "Take this."

She laughs softly, though it sounds almost affectionate. "In the future, 'cool' means something is good or interesting."

"I see."

Kylie turns in a half-circle, studying the walls, and the images painted on them, no doubt. "What is all this? It looks old. I mean, older than the nineteenth century."

"It is very old, yes." I toss my coat onto the floor and come up behind her, settling my hands on her shoulders. "The Outlands was once inhabited by a native tribe called the Kev-itash, and this was their most sacred place."

"When did they leave? You said 'once' they lived here."

"They vanished long ago before the first European explorers set foot on the continent. I heard the tale from an elder of the Ute tribe whom I encountered during my journey to the Outlands."

She seems fascinated with the painted images on the wall, so much so that she hasn't yet complained about my hands resting on her shoulders. "Why did you come here? I mean, you're from England. Why move all the way to the Wild West?"

"To explain, I need to tell you the legend that the Ute elder shared with me and how it relates to my past."

Why do I want to tell her? It does not matter. But deep down, I feel that she needs to know everything if I'm to protect her from the worst elements in the Outlands—and from the wolf within me. I cannot explain why I believe this, but it feels vital that I share everything with this woman, in this place, at this moment.

"Sit down," I tell her. "The story will take time to relate."

I take her hand, leading her to a spot where several blankets have been folded and laid atop each other to form a sort of mattress. To my surprise, when I gesture for her to sit there, she does so without complaint or eye-rolling. I light a fire in the blackened, sunken circle that has previously hosted fires. I'd left twigs and branches here for that purpose as well as a piece of flint.

Kylie watches me striking the flint until sparks fly and the twigs ignite.

When I take a seat beside her, I leave a discreet gap between our bodies.

"You've been here a lot, huh?" she says. "You've got a comfy place to sit and a kind of fire pit." She wrinkles her nose. "But where will the smoke go? We might suffocate."

I point straight up. "You can't see it from down here, but there is a narrow, natural chimney above us. The sun can't reach this far down, but the smoke wends its way out."

She gazes up, seeming transfixed by the idea of what lies above us.

"Are you sure you're not cold?" I ask.

"Positive." She looks at me. "I want to hear your story."

Never have I shared the tale with anyone. But I know, in a way I can't explain or hope to understand, that the time has come to expose all my secrets.

To her.

CHAPTER TEN

Nathaniel
Six years ago

I APPROACH THE FRONT STEPS OF THE TOWERING BOX OF A HOUSE that hunkers before me, its walls constructed from the darkest grey bricks. The tall, narrow windows do nothing to alleviate the unrelenting darkness of this place. It does not help that I have arrived after nightfall. A waxing moon glows in the sky, its face nearly full but not quite. I wipe sweat from my brow. I'd ridden in a wagon with a farmer until we reached a crossroads three miles from where I stand now, then walked the rest of the way as the sun sank lower and lower.

My father summoned me, but he cared nothing for how I got here.

Or *if* I got here, I'm sure. He would have been quite happy if highwaymen had murdered me.

The last words my mother ever spoke to me echo through my thoughts. *Don't trust him, Nathaniel, that man is the devil himself.*

But my mother is dead. I have nowhere to go except to my father, who claimed he wished for me to come here. So I mount the steps and rap on the huge doors.

They swing open a moment later, and a grey-haired man rakes his gaze over me, his lip curling faintly. "Lord Wilderhampton will see you in the drawing room."

I remove my hat. "Ah, thank you, sir. I've had a long journey and would appreciate the chance to sit down."

"You will not sit while in this house." He sniffs, his lip curling even more. "Follow me."

Though I've tried desperately to shed my lower-class accent, at my mother's behest, I can't rid myself of it entirely. That's why the butler, or whatever this man is, gives me haughty, disgusted looks as I follow him into the house. My clothing doesn't help matters. It had started out clean, if not fashionable, but the long journey from London has left them rumpled and somewhat dirty, and a slight odor might be wafting off me. I've gotten used to the curled-lip treatment from folk who think I am beneath them. A butler is above me? I suppose he is, considering that he's in the service of an earl.

I am nothing but a commoner.

The butler ushers me into the drawing room and leaves, shutting the doors.

What am I meant to do? Wait here for my father, I assume. This room has a couch and chairs, as well as a fireplace. No flames burn in the hearth, though. I'm cold, and I wonder if I should start a fire. Probably not. This isn't my home, after all.

The doors swing inward, and Mordecai Fortescue, fifth Earl of Wilderhampton, enters the drawing room and halts just inside the doorway. He walks with a cane, which I hadn't seen him do the last time we'd met. That had been eight months ago. He seems much older now, his cheekbones more prominent and his eyes sunken while his frame appears more fragile. His shoulders are sloped and hunched forward, while he seems to breathe harder than necessary.

"What a pleasure it is to cast my gaze upon my son," he says, though his caustic tone belies the politeness of his words. "You look every bit the guttersnipe, don't you? Can't manage to bathe or wash your clothing before entering the house of an earl."

"I apologize, Father," I say, twisting my hat in my hands. "I couldn't afford a carriage, so I had to—"

"Do you think I care about your troubles?" He lifts his chin to glare down at me over the tip of his nose. "Your mother should have provided for you better."

Charlotte Wilson had been a farmer's daughter—a good, kind woman—when she met Mordecai Fortescue. He'd seen her tending her family's garden while he rolled by in his carriage. The newly titled Earl of Wilderhampton had stopped to speak to the farm girl who knew nothing of the upper classes and what their kind could do to an innocent like her. My father swept her off her feet with romantic promises of marriage and the aristocratic life. Once he'd seduced her, though, he reneged on those vows. He bedded her once and walked away.

Then my mother discovered she was with child. Her parents took her to Wilderhampton and dumped her on the front steps, then they went home.

What did my father do? He took her as his mistress, installing her in a simple flat in London where he would visit for the sole purpose of shagging her. Eventually, he decided it would be a wonderful joke if he married my mother and made me legitimate, solely to enrage his uncles and cousins and whatever other relatives he had left.

I never met any of them. This is my first time at Wilderhampton.

"Begging pardon, sir," I say, though I loathe using the word sir to refer to him. "I wondered why you bid me come to you."

"Careful, boy," he says in a sharp tone. "Your guttersnipe pedigree is burrowing back into your voice. I ordered Charlotte to teach you to speak like a gentleman, but I imagine it was too much of a strain for her to do so since she was a guttersnipe too."

Neither I nor my mother was ever indigent, but I see no point in reminding him of that. Lord Wilderhampton knows this already. He despises anyone who is not of his class, though, and facts matter little to him.

My father shuffles toward the couch.

When I try to help him, he swats my hands away and glowers at me.

Once he has settled onto the couch, I move toward a chair.

"You will stand," he commands. "Only members of the beau monde dare to sit in my presence."

I stand near the end of the couch, hat in my hands, head bowed. I can still see him, despite lowering my head.

"That's more like it," he says. "At least Charlotte taught you to show a little deference. Now, to the matter at hand. Firstly, I have chosen a bride for you."

"What?" My head snaps up, but I quickly lower it again. "I meant, ah, Mother never mentioned that to me."

"Of course not. I didn't choose your bride until after Charlotte passed on." He lays a hand on his chest, breathing more heavily, then clears his throat. "On to the second item of news. I've devised a grand farce as my last act before I die."

"A farce? You mean to stage a play?"

"No, you ignorant squit." He leans toward me, his eyes gleaming with a dark humor that matches his smile. "I mean to scandalize the beau monde and especially my brothers. Barnabas and Archibald will be apoplectic over this, and my only regret is that I won't be here to witness their choleric tantrums."

"I don't understand."

"Of course you don't. Allow me to explain." He grins, but there is nothing cheery about it. "I made you my legitimate heir when I wed Charlotte. No one knows of that union yet, though. When I die, my title and this estate will fall to you."

"What? No, I can't—"

"Silence, boy." He thumps his cane on the floor. "I have already set these plans in motion. My grand farce will unfold soon enough, as my health wanes daily. I'm ready to meet St. Peter or whatever demon might steal my soul first. My brothers will pound their fists on my casket when they learn a guttersnipe like you has become the sixth Earl of Wilderhampton. Just wait until Barnabas and Archibald learn that I've installed a street urchin as my heir."

He laughs like the devil himself.

Neither I nor my mother has ever been a street urchin, but he does not care about the truth. I know my father will never approve of my vocation since I work as a blacksmith, so I don't mention it.

While I wring my hat in my hands, I swallow against the tightness in my throat. Inheriting a title and an estate sounds wonderful, but no one in the aristocracy will ever accept me. And as for my uncles... If they are anything like my father, they will stop at nothing to get rid of me.

I swallow again, but my throat grows tighter. "I thought only sons could inherit titles, not brothers."

"That shows how ignorant you truly are. The letters patent for the earldom of Wilderhampton specify that brothers may inherit if no legitimate heir survives the earl or if that heir dies after succeeding him."

Which means my uncles may murder me and acquire the title and the estate.

My father rises, with some effort. "Now, it's time to meet your betrothed." He pounds his cane on the floor and shouts, "Bring the girl, Bateman."

A moment later, the doors open, and a young woman walks into the room.

I stare at her, the most beautiful creature I've ever seen. Her white-blonde hair seems to shimmer with an inner light, and her trim but sensual figure is accentuated by the dress she wears. She approaches us as the butler closes the doors.

Her eyes, the color of darkest whisky, focus on me. She lifts one manicured brow.

"Come, child," my father says, hobbling toward the girl to grasp her elbow and nudge her toward me. "Greet your intended. This is my son, Nathaniel. Address him as Mr. Fortescue since the urchin hardly deserves to be a viscount, despite what tradition calls for."

I'm a viscount? I suppose that's because I am the only son and heir of Lord Wilderhampton, but I never knew I'd acquired such a title.

The girl offers her delicate hand to me. "It is indeed a pleasure to meet you, Mr. Fortescue. I am Cordelia Atherton."

"She comes from superb stock," my father announces. "Her family is eminently respectable but endures financial hardship at the moment. That is the only reason I was able to arrange such a splendid match. You shall wed upon my death."

Cordelia eyes me up and down. Her nose wrinkles, and she wipes her palm on her dress as if removing filth from her skin.

Naturally, I don't understand her reaction until much later.

I cannot take my eyes off the girl, transfixed by her beauty and elegance. I remain mesmerized by Cordelia for the next nine months—or rather, I remain mesmerized by the memory of her since we don't see each other again until my father dies. Then, I become the sixth Earl of Wilderhampton, and the treachery begins. For nine months, I evade murder attempts by agents of my uncles and learn every underhanded way to survive with little money and only myself to rely on. I also learn how to fight, the dirty way. I can't be gentlemanly when assassins are after me. I also shag various women, most of whom are prostitutes, in an attempt to numb the fear and pain with sex, but it never works.

The two men who want me dead, Archibald and Barnabas, remain as ghosts to me. They act through third parties only.

By the time Mordecai Fortescue has met his demise, I am no longer the "urchin" he believed me to be. I retain a sliver of my mother's hopefulness, though, keeping it safe deep within me. But that sliver disintegrates on the night I arrive at Wilderhampton to claim my rightful place there.

Cordelia is waiting for me in the drawing room. She stands when I enter. "Lord Wilderhampton, please accept my condolences for the loss of your beloved father."

"Beloved?" I say, and even my voice has become harsher than it used to be. "I despised my father as much as he despised me. If you're here to sever our engagement, you will receive no complaint from me."

"Do you no longer wish to wed me?" she asks in a soft, beguiling voice. When she walks over to me, I smell the sweet, flowery scent that clings to her. "I still wish it... Nathaniel."

She fingers the lapels of my coat, leaning in.

Good lord, she smells wonderful. I want to shag her the way I did all those whores and trollops. But Cordelia is a proper woman, and I cannot debauch her.

"I have changed," I tell her. "You will not be marrying a sweet boy who knows nothing of the world. I'm a beast now."

No, I hadn't officially become one yet, but I believed I'd behaved like one.

She smiles. "That makes no difference to me, Nathaniel. I like forceful men."

A flash of light outside the window draws my attention, and I see it's a torch. What on earth? Who would dare trespass on Wilderhampton land?

"Wait here," I tell Cordelia. "I must go out there and chase away trespassers."

"You truly are master of Wilderhampton, aren't you?"

I ignore her statement and rush outside. Two people are standing at the edge of the lawn, and as I draw closer to them, I realize it's a man and a woman. The man holds the torch and is dressed in a fine suit, though he's removed his coat, which hangs over his arm. The woman dresses like the Rom girl I'd bedded a few months ago, so I assume she is a gypsy too.

"You are trespassing," I say as I halt a few yards away from them. "This is Wilderhampton land, and there are no public footpaths through this part of the estate. Please turn around and head back the way you came."

The man sniggers at me. "I am Archibald Fortescue, your uncle. This land rightfully belongs to me, not the bastard son of my wicked brother."

"I am not illegitimate. And my father expressly bequeathed his title and property to me."

"We'll see about that." Archibald glowers at the gypsy woman. "Do it."

She snarls words in another language and spits at him.

He seizes her arm, giving the woman a hard shake. "Do it, you stupid cow. I paid you handsomely for your service." When she spits again, he yanks her closer. "You know what will happen to your daughter if you refuse me."

She scowls but nods, then faces me. The woman raises her hands, shuts her eyes, and begins to chant softly in another language. A bronze medallion dangles between her fingers.

The sterile light of the full moon shines down on us, casting the scene in an eerie glow. I can't resist glancing up at the moon and its mottled face as an odd tension builds inside me. I begin to breathe harder, as if a large weight has settled onto my chest. A burning sensation prickles over my skin, beginning with my face and spreading downward through my entire body.

"What's happening?" I ask, my voice strained by the tightness in my throat. I swerve my attention to the Rom woman who still chants, though her voice is growing louder with every passing second. "What are you doing to me?"

Archibald chuckles. "The gyppo is solving a problem for me. Hurry up, you worthless hag."

Her voice resonates around us, bouncing off the house and the trees.

The burning on my skin transforms into a sensation of a million tiny insects crawling over my flesh and sinking their fangs in deep. I let out a hoarse cry and fall to my knees. My vision becomes blurry, my ears ring, and I drop forward onto my hands and knees. Pain rips through my body, down to my bones—and through them. I swear my bones are cracking and splitting.

A scream explodes out of me, its echoes drowning out the gypsy's final words.

I collapse onto the ground, flat on my face. Can't breathe. Can't hear my heartbeat. My eyes remain open, but I don't blink and can't move my eyes. Am I dead?

Archibald kneels beside me. He flips me over roughly, grasps my chin, and jostles my head. A nasty grin splits his mouth. "The gyppo did it. I will become Earl of Wilderhampton." He rises and slaps the woman's arm. "Good show. Now, it's time I consummated my betrothal to the succulent Miss Atherton."

My uncle saunters into the house.

I should get up. To protect Cordelia. From Archibald. But I can't move. My lungs have begun to work, though weakly.

The gypsy kneels beside me. "I am sorry for what I have done, but it was all I could think of to spare you the fate your uncle wished for you."

He wanted me dead. She spared me. Why? I open my mouth to ask, but all that emerges is a hoarse gasp.

"Do not attempt to speak yet," she says, her accented voice more compassionate than I would've expected. "I am no ordinary Rom, if such a thing as normal exists for my kind. I am a daughter of Erosabel. She will guide you now. Follow her call, wherever it leads."

The gypsy rises and disappears into the trees.

A scream reverberates inside the house, penetrating the drawing-room window to reach my ears.

Cordelia.

I clamber to my feet, still feeling a bit shaky, and stagger toward the house. Did that scream sound angry rather than terrified? I can't think well enough to distinguish between the two.

A figure races out of the front doors, careening toward me.

"Nathaniel!" Cordelia shouts. "Where are you, Nathaniel?"

I move out of the shadows of the trees and stumble forward. "Cordelia, are you injured?"

She reaches me and throws her arms around my neck. "No, I'm all right. But your uncle…" She pulls back just enough that we can look at each other. "He tried to violate me, but I struck him over the head with a large candlestick."

"He deserved that."

She takes two steps backward, straightens her dress, and lifts her chin. "I've killed him."

"You had no choice. It was not your fault."

The moon bathes us in its glow.

I tilt my head back to gaze at it, and a strange longing rises inside me. No, not longing. The need pulses deep inside me, growing stronger with every second that I stare at the moon. I feel connected to it somehow, as if I have become one with the milky orb suspended above me. My breaths come faster and harder. I clench my fists.

And growl softly.

"Nathaniel?" Cordelia says. "What are you doing?"

My cock thickens and throbs. I grit my teeth and lower my gaze to Cordelia. Those breasts, those hips, that mouth. I need to consume her in every way imaginable, and I can't keep from growling through my gritted teeth.

She watches me without expression.

"Run," I snarl. "Get away from me, as far as possible."

Her blank expression transforms into a sensual smile. "I'm not afraid of you, Nathaniel. I told you, I like rough men."

"Something has happened to me. I can't—I might—I need to fuck you."

"Good." She unties the laces on her bodice and yanks it open, revealing her naked breasts. "I removed my corset while I was waiting for you because I prayed you would debauch me tonight. Do it, Nathaniel. Take me like an animal."

There's wanton hunger in her voice.

I shouldn't do what she wants. But I need to. No, I am not a beast. Yet I feel like one. Savage. Ravenous. Ready to mate.

She removes her dress.

And I pounce on her like a wild animal, clawing and clutching at her without a thought for her well-being. By the time I realize she has stopped moving, I've done what the beast within demanded. I've defiled her. More than that, I have...killed her.

My heart pounds as I note her closed eyes and the red streaks of blood from the claw marks I inflicted on her delicate body. I am a monster. That gypsy might've spared me from death, but she has cursed me with something far worse.

I abscond into the forest, never to return to Wilderhampton.

CHAPTER ELEVEN

Kylie

WOW, THAT'S ONE INCREDIBLE STORY. I CAN'T BELIEVE HE NOT ONLY told me all of that but also shared how it affected him emotionally. His expression stayed stoic the entire time, though his feelings colored his voice. I met this man yesterday, and yet I feel like I've known him for a lot longer, especially after everything he's told me.

Maybe I've misjudged him. I mean, he has protected me in his own way, and he just spilled his guts to me. Considering how awful his life has been so far, I'm beginning to understand why he behaves the way he does.

He's scared. And lonely.

But I don't think he's done with his story yet.

"How did you end up here, in this town?" I ask. "The gypsy cursed you, then you ran away. What happened after that?"

Nathaniel is leaning against the wall, but he keeps his face turned away from me. "The Rom witch had urged me to follow Erosabel's call, and so I heeded her. For months, I did whatever it took to reach my destination, though I had no idea where I might end up. The call was more akin to a magnetic pull, tugging me in the right direction. I stowed away on a steamship headed to America. I'll spare you the details of my travails. When I finally reached the Utah Territory, I was drawn to an area that I discovered is inhabited by the Ute, and I met an elder who told me the story of Erosabel."

Yeah, I remember he mentioned that Ute elder earlier. His tale fascinates me and also makes me want to hug him. I don't think he'd appreciate that, though.

Nathaniel bows his head, staring down at his hands. "This is the story. Many centuries ago, Erosabel was a Rom girl who was captured by Zor'imuth, a demon prince, and forced to become his mistress against her will. She managed to escape, but the prince was ruthless and determined to recapture her. The only way her family could ensure her safety was to send her out to sea on a raft and pray the gods would protect her. When she reached what would later be known as the New World, she wandered for years in search of a safe home. Eventually, Erosabel made her way west, where she met a Kevitash warrior called Rohnesh, and they fell in love."

"How romantic. But I'm guessing things went south."

"Yes." He turns his face to me, his expression stony. "Erosabel and Rohnesh bore children, and their life was a happy one for years—until Zor'imuth tracked her down."

Why do I feel anxious all of a sudden? I guess I'm identifying with Erosabel a little too much. Not that I've ever been kidnapped by a demon prince. But I am trapped in a creepy town with a sexy but grumpy werewolf.

Nathaniel heaves himself off the makeshift mattress and offers me his hand. "Let me show you the rest."

I take his hand, accepting his help in getting up, and let him lead me to the wall on the other side of the chamber where stylized drawings have been painted on the stone.

He moves behind me, laying his hands on my shoulders. His body brushes against me as he speaks in a hushed voice that captivates me. "These drawings relate the story of Erosabel and Rohnesh. Look at the images. Don't think, simply let them penetrate your mind, and the story will unfold before your eyes."

I can't stop myself from leaning into him, letting my head fall back against his chest as I gaze at the drawings. The figures depicted are composed of black and red paint. The longer I stare at them, the more I relax against Nathaniel and let myself sort of...drift away. I feel almost lightheaded, though his hands ground me, and just like he said, the story unfolds before my eyes. The figures painted on the rock surface begin to move while noises echo softly in my ears. The sound of drums and chanting resonates through me at first, then I hear a deep, feral growling noise.

The pictures dance across the rough stone surface.

Erosabel and Rohnesh are walking with their children when a demon leaps in front of them, snarling and gnashing his teeth. This is Zor'imuth, the demon prince who enslaved Erosabel. She recognizes him and hugs her children to her breast, but the demon wants his property back and will stop at nothing to have her. Rohnesh attacks Zor'imuth but is grievously injured. To save the man she loves and their children, Erosabel agrees to go with the demon provided he heals Rohnesh and vows never to come near him or her children again and never to harm them in any way.

But Erosabel has a secret plan, one that she enacts as soon as Zor'imuth agrees to her terms. She gathers all the magics of both the Rom and Rohnesh's people to cast a hideous curse on the demon prince. From this day forward, Zor'imuth will be as a human man, but one cursed to hold a ravenous wolf spirit inside him. Not only will he suffer all the weaknesses of a mortal, but he will also harbor those of a wolf.

The cost of laying down the curse is hefty for Erosabel. It drains the life from her body, though not her soul. That lives on. With her last breath, she gifts her daughter with a medallion forged by magic that holds within it the very essence of the curse. The curse also exacts a toll on the Kevitash, who may have no more children. Their line dies out, except for Rohnesh and his brothers, whose descendants live on through their connection with the Rom.

The figures on the wall stop moving.

I blink rapidly, swaying a touch, and little by little I rouse from the trance those images had created.

A woman's voice whispers in my mind, as gently as a breeze. *The choice is yours, daughter, and yours alone. That is my gift to you. Save it for the one who needs it the most.*

Nathaniel bends his head to murmur in my ear, "The rest of the story was told to me by the Ute elder. When Rohnesh's tribe learned of Erosabel's spell, both she and

Rohnesh were banished. His brothers went with them, and together, they made their way back to the Old World and Erosabel's people. Their lineage lived on, and all female children are known as the Daughters of Erosabel."

"What does this have to do with you?"

"The gypsy who cursed me was a Daughter of Erosabel, but I still do not understand the full import of that fact. I was drawn to the Outlands, and to this cavern. It means something, that is all I know."

Was the voice that whispered to me a moment ago the voice of Erosabel? Yesterday, I would've balked at the idea. But since then, I've been dragged back in time and met a werewolf. I can no longer deny anything simply because it seems impossible.

If it had been Erosabel who whispered to me, then she was referring to *me* as her daughter. The shaman had called me the keeper of the wolf's destiny. Erosabel also said I should save my gift for the one who needs it the most.

Oh no, no, no. I can't be—I mean, that's crazy. I am not destined to save Nathaniel or to be with him. What gift am I supposed to give him, anyway? I don't have magic, so I can't de-curse him. I don't see what else I could give him. Maybe the voice in my head meant the medallion. But no, when Nathaniel took that, it set his pants on fire.

Maybe I have to give it to him.

I pull the medallion out of my pocket, turn around, and hold out my hand, palm up, with the bronze disk lying on it. "Here. I'm giving you this as a gift."

He arches one brow, then eyes the medallion. "The last time I touched that, it burned me."

"Try it again. I'm gifting it to you."

Despite still seeming dubious, he takes the object between his thumb and forefinger.

And it bursts into flames.

Nathaniel shouts and drops the medallion. He cradles his formerly flaming hand in his other palm. "What the bloody hell was that? Why did you want to burn me?"

"I didn't. I'm sorry, that was a dumb idea. I just thought—" I snatch up the medallion, stuffing it in my pocket. "Never mind. I'm so sorry. Are you okay?"

He compresses his lips. "I will survive."

While I gaze at him, at his stoic expression and the pain in his eyes, I try to imagine what it must feel like to be cursed. I know the gypsy woman did that to save his life, but she's left him with a condition that keeps him separate from the rest of the world, out of fear that he might hurt someone else the way he unintentionally hurt his fiancée. Ever since I turned up in the Outlands, and we've developed this weird connection, he's even more scared.

Of course, being a man, he refuses to acknowledge that anxiety and gets grumpy instead.

I want to help him, and I don't think that's because of the medallion, the images on the wall, or any prophecy or curse. I like him. And oddly, I trust him.

"We should leave," he says. "If I'm away from town for too long, the locals run wild."

"Okay. But answer one question first. Why do you stay in the Outlands?"

"I have no choice."

"Why not?" I move closer, our bodies inches apart, and tip my head back to see his face. "Why can't you just leave?"

His expression hardens, and his tone turns icy. "No one leaves the Outlands unless they're in a pine box."

A coffin, he means. The only way out is to die?

"I don't understand," I say. "Does the curse keep you here?"

"Not the wolf curse, but the power of whatever or whoever created this place. The Devil's Outlands is not a simple town in the Utah Territory. It is a piece of Hell that burst out into the mortal world."

"Have you tried to leave?"

"Yes." He grasps my upper arms. "I was thrown back inside. Ricocheted off the boundary, in fact. It is an invisible barrier that encloses the town, this butte, and the surrounding area."

Oh, fabulous. I'm trapped in a pocket of Hell.

Maybe the prophecy means I can break us both out of here. Somehow. I wish this stuff came with explicit instructions instead of unhelpful vagueness.

"If I could send you home," he says, his voice rough with emotion, "I would do it. Everyone in the Outlands was consigned here because they committed a terrible act. We belong in purgatory. But you...” He shakes his head the tiniest bit. “You do not belong here.”

But I think I do. I belong with *him*. Maybe.

Despite my confusion about the prophecy, I know one thing for certain. I want to be with him. Right now. In this cavern.

I splay my hands on his chest and glide them up to his neck, clasping them behind his nape. “Make love to me, Nathaniel.”

“I can’t. The wolf inside me—”

“Doesn’t control you. I’ve seen you tighten the leash on it, so I know you can.” I wrap my arms around his neck and mold my body to his. God, I love the feel of all those muscles and the heat of his body. “I know you won’t hurt me, but however you need to take me, do it. I’m stronger than I look.”

“The last time I shagged a woman, I mauled her to death.”

I’m not sure that’s what happened since he doesn’t remember. But I am sure, for no logical reason at all, that he would never hurt me. “Please, Nathaniel, I want to be with you.”

“Are you... Ah, have you been with...”

“Yes, Nathaniel, I’m a virgin.” Because I’ve been waiting for him, though I can’t prove that. Science went out the window the moment I was hurled backward in time and dropped into a cursed town. “I want you, so please, don’t say no.”

I press my lips to his.

He stays absolutely still for several seconds, his body stiff and unyielding. Then he slips his arms around me and drags his palms up my back, spreading his fingers. The sensation makes me shiver with anticipation, and I push my tongue between his lips only to meet the barrier of his teeth. He’s gritting them, of course. I keep flicking my tongue out to tap his teeth until, with a long groan that resonates in his chest, he surrenders to the kiss.

His tongue lashes mine, and I moan because it feels incredible. He tastes like exotic things I can’t describe, but those flavors make me so hot for him that I wrap one leg around his like I’m trying to climb onto his body. I guess I am. That’s how much I want him.

The iron-hard line of his erection is trapped between us.

He moves one hand to grip my ass, then shoves it between my cheeks. His long fingers caress me through my pants, and suddenly, I need to get naked with him. Right this minute. Can't wait any longer because I'm sure I'll lose my mind if I can't have him inside me.

I moan into his mouth.

With me latched onto him, he rushes toward the wall.

My back smacks into it.

His kiss, greedy and carnal and full of animal lust, drives out all thoughts and any shred of common sense I might've still harbored deep in my psyche. He growls softly, the sound vibrating into me. I thrust my tongue deeper, not caring that our teeth clash and I can't breathe with him devouring me so thoroughly.

Pushing a hand between us, he unfastens my pants and shoves them down to my ankles.

I thank heavens I went commando because I can't wait one millisecond longer to feel him inside me.

When he plasters me to the rock wall with his entire body, I realize his pants are gone too. From the waist down, nothing separates my body from his.

Holy shit, this is happening. I'm about to lose my virginity—to a werewolf.

CHAPTER TWELVE

Nathaniel

I CAN'T STOP THIS, NO MATTER HOW HARD I TRY. NOT THAT I AM TRYing. I can't think with her body pasted to mine and her tongue in my mouth, otherwise I would have dragged her out of here and back to town, then locked her in my bedroom and left. I haven't been with a woman in five years, and the last one I'd killed. I shouldn't do this with Kylie.

But I can't stop.

The scent of her desire permeates the air, and the sensation of her skin on mine drives me mad. The hairs between her thighs tease my flesh, but it's the slickness trickling down her skin that pushes me over the edge.

I hoist her leg and thrust inside her body, shattering her maidenhead.

She throws her head back and moans. "Yes, don't stop."

"Didn't that hurt?"

"Only for half a second. I'm good to go, so please don't stop."

I couldn't if I wanted to. Can't be gentle either, but she said she doesn't care how I take her. I had done this only once after my transformation, and the beast had taken over then. Here in this mystical place, with her, I feel no more than a hint of the wolf within, just enough to make me growl as I hoist her other leg and begin to pound into her. The sounds of our bodies merging, of our harsh breaths and my grunts, echo inside the rock chamber.

When she shouts my name, it reverberates around us.

She bounces on my cock with every thrust, giving me glimpses of the images on the wall behind her. My gaze lands on the painting of the Kevitash warrior, but it shimmers and mutates into the outline of a wolf.

That's what I am. An animal. I'm taking her like a wild beast.

I freeze, gasping for air.

Kylie stares at me, breathing hard too, her cheeks flushed. "Why did you stop?"

"Because I—I might hurt you."

"I'm fine. Please keep going."

"Not like this." I scuffle backward and drop down onto the cushion of blankets on my back. She lies atop me, and my cock is still nestled inside her. "I need you to do this for me. Move, Kylie, take command."

"Of you?"

"Yes. Please."

She lifts her head off my chest. "But I don't know how."

I run my hands up and down her arms. "You do know. It's instinct, that's all. Sit up and rock your hips, then let your body show you what to do."

Biting her lip, she pushes up with her hands on my chest until she sits astride me.

"Go on," I say. "Have your way with me."

She hesitates only for a heartbeat, then she slides off me to kick her boots off and discard her clothing.

My God, she's beautiful. Her nipples jut from the dusky pink flesh that surrounds them, and when she skims a hand over her flat belly, my gaze follows that motion down to her navel, and further to the thatch of hairs between her thighs. Her creamy skin has the faintest freckles scattered here and there, though not on her face or those tempting breasts.

Kylie kneels over me, eying my shaft like she's not sure what to do with it.

I take her hand, guiding it down to my length and folding her fingers around it. "Grasp me while you take my cock inside you."

She nods, then does what I said, easing her body down inch by inch while my shaft slides deeper and deeper into her channel, the silky, smooth walls conforming to my flesh. It feels so bloody wonderful that I never want the sensation to stop.

But now that she has my length seated inside her, she seems in need of more encouragement.

"Move your hips, love," I say. "Do what feels right."

Laying her palms on my chest, she rocks her hips gently. The way she keeps hold of her lip, captured between her teeth, makes me need to pound into her like a beast again, but I don't want her first sexual experience to be like that. The first time I'd bedded a woman, it was not gentle. The whore I'd hired enjoyed rough sex, and after that, the many attempts on my life had hardened my heart and my soul. I'd never wanted intimacy. But with Kylie, I do want it.

Am I capable of that anymore?

The woman riding me bites her lip again while she carefully unbuttons my shirt and spreads the halves wide to expose my skin. "Oh wow, look at these muscles." She skates her palms over my chest and bends down to drag her tongue across it too, all while still rolling her hips into me in a steady rhythm. "God, you're hot, Nathaniel."

I've decided to assume "hot" is a compliment and means she likes my body. "You are the most beautiful and bewitching woman in the world, Kylie."

She licks a path up to my throat, pausing there while her heated breaths reflect off my skin. When her tongue curls around my earlobe, I hiss in a breath and seize her hips. Bloody hell, she's going to summon the beast if she doesn't stop tormenting me this way, but I can't help loving the way it feels every time any part of her touches me. She grips my shoulders and straightens her arms, lifting herself off my chest.

And she moves faster.

Her body rises slightly every time she rolls her hips forward. The delicate sensation of her hairs teasing my skin and her arse grazing my thighs heightens my need, but despite the beast craving more, I push it back into the recesses of my mind. I want to savor this time with her, not satisfy my own needs at the expense of hers.

When was the last time I'd thought of a woman's pleasure above my own?

Never. Not until today.

Kylie quickens her pace, her breathing accelerating too in time with her movements. She throws her head back, her eyes half-closed, and lets her mouth fall open as her lips curl into an erotic smile of sheer bliss. Her breasts sway every time she rocks forward.

I can't catch my breath. She's beautiful, sensual, brave, and wonderful. The need to spill my seed within her body grows stronger every moment, and I know I can't hold it back much longer.

She cups her breasts and flicks her thumbs over the tips.

The pressure within me grows too powerful. I can't wait, but I need her to go with me, so I reach between her thighs to rub her rigid bud. "Come for me, love, please."

Her head snaps forward, though her eyes remain closed, and she slaps her palms down on my chest. "Keep doing that. Oh God. I'm about to—"

While I keep rubbing, her entire body freezes. Her face cinches up into an expression of pain, the kind that heralds intense pleasure. The instant she comes, I flip us over and punch into her twice more while I spill myself inside her and let out a long, groaning shout that becomes a harsh howl at the very end.

I pull out of her body and roll onto my back, lying beside her. My ankles are still trapped in my trouser legs, but that fact scarcely registers in my brain.

She smiles. "Thank you, Nathaniel. That was amazing."

When I shift in place so I can tuck her against me, I notice a bit of blood on my cock. "Sorry. I hope I didn't hurt you."

"No, not in the least. But why are you apologizing?"

"I took your virginity. And I didn't even use a French letter."

"A what?"

I suppose in her time they have a different word for it. Or perhaps they don't need such things anymore. "It's a second skin that covers a man's cock to deter conception."

She clamps her lips together, clearly attempting to stifle a laugh, and ends up spluttering. "I guess you mean it's a condom, but you've probably never heard that word."

"Of course I have."

"Really? I didn't know Victorian werewolves had the same lingo as us future people, but that's cool." She dances her fingertips over my chest. "Did you howl like a wolf a minute ago? It didn't sound exactly like that, but there were similarities."

"Yes, I did howl, after a fashion."

She sits up and scans me from head to toe with her gaze. "Would you mind taking your clothes off? I'd love to get a good look at you."

"I'm lying right beside you. Look all you want."

"You're still wearing clothes. Well, sort of." She leans over me, and her lips graze mine when she speaks in a sensual tone. "Please, Nathaniel. Please, please, please."

"As you wish. But you shouldn't speak that way unless you want me to ravish you again." I sit up and remove my shirt, then shed my trousers too as well as my boots and socks. Once I've discarded all my clothing, I lie back down with my hands clasped under my head. "Are you happy now?"

"Oh yeah." She pores her gaze over the length and breadth of me, her lips ticking upward a touch, then she glances at me sideways. "Is this strictly a viewing, or can I feel you up too?"

My cock twitches when she asks me that, and I find I'm suddenly breathing harder. "You may touch any part of me that you wish to feel, but be forewarned, I may not be able to stop myself from shagging you once you're done fondling my body."

"Oh, darn."

I love the way she's smiling at me, the slant of her lips simultaneously teasing and amorous. But I should not let her fondle my body, considering that I have no self-control with this woman. I deflowered her moments ago, and her blood still stains my shaft. If I take her a second time, I might harm her unintentionally. She needs time to recover before I enjoy her body again.

No, I should never ravish her again. I shouldn't have done it the first time, and I will not repeat the act.

"Oh no," she moans, her posture sagging. "You're turning back into the glowering, growling sheriff, aren't you? I can tell by the way you're tensing up and clenching your jaw. There's even a teeny muscle ticking away." She stretches out a hand to tap my jaw. "Right there."

She is correct. I am tensing my entire body in anticipation—or dread, perhaps—of what I must do now.

I rise to my feet. "Get dressed. We can't stay here any longer."

Her mouth slants downward at one corner, and she blusters out a sigh. "Yeah, yeah, I know. We have to go back to that creepy-ass town, and you'll probably lock me in your bedroom again."

"I gave you the key. That means only you have the power to lock, or unlock, the door."

Once we've both reassembled our clothing, I grab my coat and grasp her hand. Her shoulders still sag as if she's disappointed or perhaps despondent at the prospect of returning to town. I snuff out the lantern and kick dirt onto the fire to douse it.

Darkness envelops us.

Unlike Kylie, I can see in the dark as well as any animal can. No, I am not human, not entirely. I still don't know what that means for me, for my future. What I do know is that I cannot have a future with Kylie. What we've just done... I should never have allowed it to happen, but I cannot erase my mistake.

As we exit the hidden passageway into the glaring sunlight, I release Kylie's hand and glance at her. She squints at the sudden brightness and can't see that I'm admiring her lovely face and her tempting body. Pressure bears down on my chest, and I tear my focus away from her as realization stabs into me like a burning, razor-sharp blade.

No, she can never be mine.

CHAPTER THIRTEEN

Kylie

ON THE TREK BACK TO TOWN, NATHANIEL DOESN'T SPEAK—NOT EVEN when I speak to him. No matter how many dumb jokes I make or how many times I teasingly tell him I'd love to lick him like a big wolfie fudge pop, he doesn't respond. Okay, maybe he didn't understand what a fudge pop is. But that doesn't fully explain his behavior. He has retreated into a distance I can't see, somewhere I can't follow him.

We just had sex, for heaven's sake. Couldn't he at least be polite?

I feel a little queasy now, and it's not only because we're getting closer and closer to town, closer and closer to the creepy residents of that town. When Nathaniel and I had made love, it had been more than a way to get off. It felt... intimate. He'd shown me how to make us both come, shown me what he liked, and known exactly what I needed. Most of the time, he's gruff and grumpy. But in that cave, he let me see another aspect of him, his tender and passionate side.

God, I love that part of him. I want him to be that way all the time, but maybe I have to accept that he has valid reasons for closing himself off.

Once we're alone in his ironclad bedroom, he'll loosen up again. Right?

The town looms not far ahead of us, maybe a hundred feet away.

A wind kicks up, swirling dust around us and fluttering his leather coat. He stares straight ahead, his eyes narrowed, and strides across the desert with all the gritty determination of a werewolf sheriff in the Wild West.

But I can't stand the quiet anymore. "Nathaniel, I—"

"Silence."

"Uh, sorry, it doesn't work that way. I'm not your prisoner or your servant." I grab his arm, yanking until he stops walking, though he doesn't look at me. "I'm the girl you screwed in a mystical cave and shared all your secrets with, so don't act like that means nothing."

A muscle jumps in his jaw.

"Talk to me, Nathaniel."

He rotates his face toward me almost in slow motion, his expression shuttered behind an impenetrable barrier. "I am afraid, child, that is exactly what it meant. Nothing. The beast in me needed a release, and I took it from the nearest available female body. If I've broken your tender heart, that's none of my concern."

My throat tightens up, and I feel the first sting of tears that want to form. No, I will not cry. No way. He looks and sounds like an unfeeling bastard, but I'm not buying it for one second. Well, okay, maybe I buy it for, like, a millisecond. I can't help feeling kind of rejected and used, but this is not the real Nathaniel Fortescue. It's his fear talking, not the man I got naked with inside a cave full of mysterious paintings that come to life.

"Don't do that," I say. "Don't shut me out because you're freaked by the fact you took my virginity. What you need to do is talk to me, not slam the door in my face."

He leans closer, and his voice becomes a wolf-like growl. "I love to fuck virgins. They're so easy to seduce and willing to do whatever depraved things I demand of them. You're fortunate I did not slake my lust the way the beast within urged me to do, or you wouldn't be standing upright, much less walking."

Yeah, I get that he's doing his damnedest to scare me, and maybe he succeeds a smidgen, but I will not let him see how much his behavior upsets me. What had I been thinking? Getting it on with a werewolf? With a man I met last night? *Jeez, Kylie, where did you leave your brain?*

In the twenty-first century, apparently.

So fine, he can have it his way. *Two can play that game, buster.*

I square my shoulders, lift my chin, and give him my best tough-chick stare. "Thank you soooo much, Sheriff Asshat, for your restraint. But I can take care of myself. And so there's no misunderstanding..." I wave my hands at my body. "You will never, never, never again get a peek at my nakedness. The only way you'll get in my pants again is if I'm dead. And FYI, the sex wasn't that great, anyway."

Maybe I overdid it a teeny bit.

So what? He's acting like a monumental dick.

I whirl away from him and stalk toward the town.

Big, bossy arms scoop me up and throw me over the shoulder of the big, bossy jerk who grabbed me. Nathaniel locks an arm around my legs. Slung over his shoulder like this, my head hangs down, and I can't see anything with my hair hanging down like a curtain.

"Put me down," I holler while kicking my feet. I can't get any leverage, though, because of the way he's got me pinned to his body.

He acts like he didn't hear me, but I know he did. A were-wolf must have doggy senses too, right? He can probably detect my heartbeat or whatever.

I can't kick him, but my arms are free. So I pound my fists into his backside.

He doesn't even flinch as far as I can tell.

I sink my teeth into his back.

Still nothing. I might as well be kicking, biting, and slug-ging a hunk of granite.

From my inverted position, I have a tough time figuring out where we're going, but I know we've entered the town. I see buildings out of the corners of my eyes. The jerk is prob-ably dragging me back to my ironclad cell. If he tries to take the key away from me, I'll bite and slug parts of him that will get his attention for sure.

His boots clomp on wooden steps as he carries me up to...somewhere. When he pushes through the swinging doors, I realize we're in the saloon.

"What happened, Lord Wolfie?" Lucy calls out. "She run away from ya? Can't blame the girl. A lowdown dirty coyote's what you are."

Nathaniel does not respond to her taunts. He carries me upstairs, taking the steps three at a time and making my head bob so much that I'm getting queasy again. Down the hall we go, and he kicks the door shut behind us.

Then, finally, he sets me down.

And I knee him in the groin. "That's for treating me like a sack of grain."

He didn't even flinch when I rammed my knee into his privates. *Damn.*

With that steely, remote expression still shuttering his features, he rakes his gaze over me. "If I require your services again, I shall make an appointment."

He stomps out the door and slams it.

I dig the key out of my pocket and lock the door. My heart is racing, and every hair on my body has stiffened, but I'm sure that's an aftereffect of our argument. When—if—Nathaniel deigns to return, I'll be giving him a supersize piece of my mind and a good old-fashioned reaming.

For what feels like ten minutes, though I can't tell the exact time without a clock or my cell phone, I pace the width of the room and fume. Pretty soon, I get sick of that. Why should I wait for Lord Asshat to come back and maybe explain himself? He probably won't, anyway. What, am I a total weakling? No, I've never been a pushover. In school, I have to fend off jerks who think they can cheat on tests by peeking over my shoulder to read my answers. Yeah, ornithology is a dog-eat-dog world.

No more pacing and waiting. I'm done with hoping Nathaniel will come to his senses, and it's time I forced him to do it.

So I leave my ironclad bedroom, locking the door behind me, and march downstairs into the saloon, heading for the exit. I pause at the bar to ask Lucy, "Do you know where Nathaniel is?"

"Nathaniel?" she says with a slight curl of her upper lip. "Lord Wolfie don't take kindly to nobody callin' him that."

"Do you know where he is?"

She shrugs. "He hightailed it outta here like he had fire ants up his caboose."

I resist the urge to give her a caustic retort and march out the door, hopping down the steps and out onto the street. Since I visited the sheriff's office earlier when I was hunting for Nathaniel, I know exactly how to get there. This time when I enter the building, I don't see a drunkard in a cell. The only living thing inside the office is the British werewolf slumped in a chair behind the desk. He holds a glass in one hand while a bottle of booze sits on the desktop. His hair is tousled like he's been running his fingers through it repeatedly, and he has his feet on the desk, ankles crossed. His leather coat hangs on a hook by the door.

I march behind his desk and perch my butt on its corner near his feet.

He eyes me over the top of his half-empty glass. "What do you want?"

"You, obviously. Why else would I traipse into your office?"

"I regret that I'm currently incapable of satisfying your lust." He swigs the rest of the golden liquid in his glass. "And I mean that quite literally."

Has stick-up-his-ass Nathaniel Fortescue gotten tipsy?

"Not here for sex," I inform him. "We are going to have a conversation."

"I regret that I'm also currently unable to satisfy that desire."

"Bullshit." I lean forward. "I'm sure you can't get it up, but you can still talk. That means you're capable of explaining yourself to me. The jig's up, Nate."

"To what jig are you referring?"

I stare straight into his eyes, feeling a touch triumphant when he squirms the tiniest bit. "I'm talking about your little scheme to convince me to go away by acting like a total dick. You had me for about five minutes. But I'm wise to your game now, so give it up."

He sets his empty glass down on the desktop and reaches for the bottle.

I snatch it away from him.

A soft growl rumbles in his throat.

"Down, boy," I snap. Then I pull the top off the bottle and sniff its contents. I almost gag just from the stench. "Whew, what on earth are you drinking?"

"The usual rotgut you'll find in a saloon. Bourbon."

"Doesn't smell anything like the bourbon I've tasted."

"It isn't for the faint of heart, which means little girls like you shouldn't try it."

Did he just issue a challenge? Probably not on purpose, but I know he's trying to insult and intimidate me as part of his desperate ploy to make me go away. *Give it up, wolfman.* Just to be contrary, I swig a mouthful of bourbon from the unmarked bottle.

And I start coughing. Hacking, actually. Fire scorches down my throat, and the liquid overpowers my senses with its acrid overtones and sour undertones. Is this bourbon or gasoline? How can any human being drink this?

Nathaniel is smirking.

Oh, you rotten bastard. He's enjoying it and feeling smugly certain that I'm too much of a sissy girl to handle the rotgut he consumes. But now that the liquid fire has settled in my belly, I decide to give it one more try. This time, I anticipate the burn as I take another swig.

No coughing. Wow, I swallowed that swill without hacking up my guts.

I smack the bottle down on the desk. My voice comes out a little hoarse. "What's the big deal? I've had vodka with Tabasco sauce in it, so this stuff is nothing."

But yeah, I am feeling a touch woozy. It'll pass in a minute, I'm sure.

Nathaniel studies me for a few seconds, then he sighs. "You truly are the most vexing woman I've ever met."

"You're the most vexing man I've ever met, so we're even."

He pulls his feet off the desk and rises, leaning in to tower over me. "I've told you the truth, Kylie. Sooner or later, the beast in me will devour you in every possible way."

Warmth shimmers through me, and my breath catches. Maybe I wouldn't mind being devoured by Nathaniel Fortescue—again. Even if that means he sinks his claws and his teeth into me.

CHAPTER FOURTEEN

Nathaniel

KYLIE DRUMMOND MUST BE INSANE SINCE NO OTHER EXPLANATION fits the facts, but I can't believe she's a lunatic. No woman on earth would want to be with a man who growls and snarls and locks himself inside a bedroom that has iron-reinforced walls. No woman with a modicum of sense would give herself to a werewolf. Yet Kylie has done precisely that. Even knowing about my past has failed to convince her to stay away from me.

I can't even hide in the Kevitash cave. Kylie knows where it is.

Why did I take her there?

Standing so close to her, I battle against the urge to drag her body into mine, kiss her, and then yank her trousers down to her ankles so I can sink my cock inside her body one more time. I've never met a woman like her before. Perhaps that explains why I have such trouble resisting her. When I had been a simple blacksmith, women evinced no interest in me. I had been polite but reserved, afraid to ask a girl to share a mug of beer with me, much less allow me to court her.

Kylie fixes her level gaze on me.

I cannot under any circumstances court her. I cannot lie with her either. The only sensible course of action is to chase her away, but I've failed at that. Perhaps I need to try an altogether different tactic and...be honest with her.

She stretches out a hand to my face and touches her finger to the spot between my eyebrows. "You're all crinkly there. Seems like you do that when you're perplexed and angry at the same time."

"I am not angry. I might be perplexed, but for the most part, I'm resigned."

"You're quitting being sheriff?"

"No, I meant I've resigned myself to...you."

She laughs delicately. "You have the cutest stuffy way of talking sometimes."

I grasp her shoulders and stare into her eyes, praying she will listen and understand what I need to tell her. "I am a wolf, Kylie, and tonight is the full moon."

"Uh-huh. Are you going to turn into an actual wolf?"

"Perhaps."

She tips her head to the side, her gaze fastened to mine. "Why does it sound like you have no idea whether you become a real wolf?"

"Because I do have no idea." I veer my gaze away from hers. "The gypsy who cursed me did not stay to explain how this works. Since I can't see myself while the transformation occurs, I haven't a clue what I look like during or after. In the morning, I awaken alone in the Kevitash cave."

"Seriously?" She pats my chest. "Don't worry. I'll watch, and after, I'll tell you what happened."

I jerk away from her. "No, Kylie, you cannot be there. It's far too dangerous."

The obstinate woman jumps off the desk and stabs a finger into my chest repeatedly while she speaks. "I am not a wimpy little girl who can't handle the sight of...whatever you turn into. I'm a strong, independent woman. If I can fend off obnoxious college boys, I can deal with a werewolf. Trust me, twenty-first century guys are way worse than you."

"Will you never listen to me?" My heart has begun to race, and an icy chill rushes through my veins. Is this panic? I've experienced such an emotion before, but never as powerfully as I feel it now. "Please heed me on this. Tonight, you must stay in my room above the saloon with the door locked."

"No."

I grip my head with both hands as if that will squeeze the solution to this problem out of my mind. "You know what I've done. I murdered my fiancée. Ripped her to ribbons and violated her body, then I left her there to die."

Kylie stands perfectly still, all expression vacating her features. After a moment, she tips her head to the side again, but this time her eyes narrow. "Hang on, wolfman. When we were in that cave, you told me you killed your fiancée, and you just said that again. But right after you announced 'I murdered my fiancée,' you said you left her to die."

"I recall the words I spoke."

"Yeah, but that doesn't make sense. You can't murder her, then leave her to die. You've got it backwards." She squints harder at me. "Did you check if she was alive or dead? Or did you assume you had killed her?"

Evading her gaze, I scratch my neck and fight the impulse to seize the bottle of bourbon and pour the contents down my throat. "I might have, well, assumed she was no longer living. You cannot understand what that night was like for me. Once the transformation began, I couldn't think or control my actions. Since then, I've learned to harness the wolf within to a certain degree, but I still have no memory of what happens when it takes over."

"Uh-*huh*," she says. "So basically, you have no idea what you look like when you become a wolf or what you do during that time, and for all you know, your fiancée is alive and kicking."

"No, she can't be. You didn't see the blood. Cordelia was—" I cover my eyes with my palms, curling my fingers into my forehead. "There was so much blood."

"Yeah, that's what happens you maul someone." Kylie pries my hands away from my eyes with her fingers. "There is a solution."

Coldness shivers through me again, raising the hairs on my arms and at my nape. "No, Kylie, you will not—"

"Shut up, Nathaniel. The guy who said nasty things to me in an idiotic attempt to dump me when I'm not even his girlfriend does not get a say in anything anymore."

I knife my fingers through my hair and shake my head, but I know I cannot dissuade her. And she's right. I have treated her abominably, which leaves me with one choice. "I apologize for my behavior earlier. It was inexcusable."

"Wrong again. It was totally excusable, and I accept your apology." She kisses my cheek. "Thank you for that."

"How can you forgive the way I treated you?"

"Because I know you're terrified. Of pretty much everything, but mostly me." She slaps a hand over my mouth when I try to speak. "Shush. I'm going with you tonight, end of discussion."

I peel her hand away from my lips. "If I can't stop you, then I will arm you."

"With what? You don't have a gun on your hip like sheriffs in movies always do."

She has mentioned "movies" before, but I decided against requesting an explanation of the term. I will not ask this time either since the answer does not matter. We have more urgent problems to consider.

I approach the locked cabinet in the corner and retrieve a rifle. Returning to Kylie, I hand her the weapon. "This is a Winchester '73 repeater. Have you ever fired a gun before?"

"Does shooting fake ducks at a carnival count?"

"I hope you were adept at hitting the targets."

She smiles with her lips sealed, forming dimples in her cheeks, and seems quite proud of herself. "I always won a prize."

"Good. This afternoon, I will instruct you on how to take down a powerful animal with this rifle. You may need to at least subdue me once the full moon rises."

"You want me to shoot you?"

I grasp her upper arms and pull her closer. "Listen to me, Kylie. You will be in danger once the beast within me awakens. This weapon may be your only salvation. If I threaten you in any manner, if I so much as growl, you must shoot me."

"But—"

"On this matter, heed me. Please."

She pats the barrel of the rifle, which she holds with the muzzle down, aimed at the floor beside our feet. "I'll do what you say, I promise."

"Thank you, Kylie."

She nudges me with her elbow. "Thank *you* for not calling me 'child' or 'creature' anymore."

"I won't use either of those terms again. You are not a silly girl." I cradle her face in my hands and brush my lips over hers. "You are a force to be reckoned with."

"You bet your ass I am."

Whistles and catcalls erupt outside.

I glance toward the doorway. "What on earth?"

Kylie sets the rifle down on the desk. "Sounds like Sheriff Nathaniel Fortescue is needed outside. Better check it out, huh?"

"Yes." I start for the door, then hesitate. "Is there the slightest chance you might stay here?"

"What do you think?"

"Stay beside me, at least."

Kylie salutes me. "Aye-aye, captain."

We hurry outside, where a crowd has gathered in the street and on the porches of the saloon and the general store. Men shout various taunts and make various unseemly noises.

"Hey there, princess, need a hand? I got two of 'em for ya."

"Nah, she wants to come over here and take a gander at the snake in my pants."

Is that the best these vulgarians can do? I search the crowd to find the woman they seem to be harassing. We must have a new arrival.

A figure marches straight through the crowd, emerging several yards away from where Kylie and I stand at the bottom of the steps outside the sheriff's office.

The woman smooths her hands over the waist of her stylish grey dress. "Nathaniel, darling, there you are. Don't be unfriendly. Come, kiss your fiancée's hand."

She holds her hand out, tipped down.

I can't move, can't stop staring at her. "Cordelia? What—How—"

"Do try to shake off the shock, darling." While still holding her hand out to be kissed, she swerves her attention to Kylie. Cordelia's brows rise gradually as she sweeps her gaze over my companion. "Is this boy your valet?"

Boy? Anyone can see Kylie has breasts.

Kylie sets her hands on her hips. "Are you Nathaniel's scullery maid?"

"His what?" Cordelia says in the haughtiest tone I have ever heard. "I am the daughter of Thomas Atherton."

"Don't think anybody around here is impressed by that." Kylie pretends to examine Cordelia with deep interest. "You don't look half bad for a shredded corpse."

Cordelia's eyes narrow, and she takes one step toward Kylie.

I seize Cordelia's arm to stop her, then grit my teeth as I force myself to speak softly. "Not out here."

The last thing I need is for the townsfolk to witness whatever Cordelia and I say to each other. I can't leave Kylie out here alone, though, which leaves me with one choice.

I seize her hand while keeping hold of Cordelia's arm and drag them both into the sheriff's office.

CHAPTER FIFTEEN

Kylie

CORDELIA ATHERTON IS A BITCH. I NEVER CALL OTHER WOMEN THAT, but I can't *not* call her an insulting name. She waltzed into town and started calling Nathaniel "darling," then she turned her perfect little nose up at me and asked if I'm a boy. Yeah, the B-word was made for her. Maybe I'm a teeny bit jealous, but that has no bearing on my opinion of the woman.

Nathaniel hauls us both into the sheriff's office and slams the door.

His jaw is so tight I bet he could grind diamonds into dust with his teeth. I swear his eyes have gotten darker and glint menacingly in the sunlight that comes in through the windows. He fists his hands at his sides.

And he stares at Cordelia.

Is he glaring? Or could that be shock? I hope it's not happy shock, like he wants to get back together with her. Why did she have to show up now? Nathaniel and I have a connection, one I don't understand but that I want to hold on to, and the sudden appearance of his former fiancée is the last thing I need.

Since the man I had sex with this morning seems incapable of speaking, I decide to do it for him. "So, Cordelia, how did you survive being mauled? Nathaniel assumed you were dead."

The woman gives me a haughty glance, then moves closer to Nathaniel. She lays a hand on his chest. "Darling, could we speak alone? Your boy servant makes me uncomfortable."

Boy? Servant? Oh, I want to slug her so hard.

Nathaniel grasps her wrist, wrenching her hand away from his chest, and pushes Cordelia away. "Kylie is not a boy, as anyone can tell since she has a bosom."

"Does she?" Cordelia throws me another snooty glance. "I hardly noticed. But I do need to speak with you alone, darling. I have much to tell you."

"Anything you want to say to me, you can say to Kylie as well."

"Why do you insist upon having your charwoman—"

"She is not my servant," Nathaniel snarls. "Enough, Cordelia. Tell me how you came to be in the Outlands."

"Oh, but that is a long story. Might I have a glass of port first?"

"Port? This is not a gentleman's drawing room. You are in purgatory, and I want to know why."

"All right, if you wish to be tiresome, I will tell you." She sashays behind the desk and settles her rump on the chair. "I assume you believed I had died. Your uncle assumed you were dead, despite the lack of bodily remains, but he found me only half-dead. So he summoned a doctor to tend to my wounds. While I convalesced, he sought out the gypsy hag and demanded proof of your demise. She told him that your remains had melted into the earth. Dear Archibald, being a profoundly stupid man, believed her story."

Nathaniel stands as stiff and unmoving as a mountain, his face impassive, tension evident in his slightly hunched shoulders and his fisted hands.

"Your uncle became hopelessly infatuated with me," Cordelia says. "He would stand to inherit your father's fortune since you had apparently died, so I allowed Archibald to wed me."

"What?" A hint of surprise flashes on Nathaniel's face, but it dissipates quickly. "Why would you do that?"

She laughs, though it's not a happy sound. "Why do you think? Your father's will permitted his eldest brother to inherit his fortune upon your death. I married Archibald, but he lasted only three months before I had to slip arsenic into his tea. He had failed to produce an heir, and I could not stand for that. Dear Archie had trouble, shall we say, hoisting the flag." She sighs, then waves a hand dismissively. "After that, I wed your Uncle Barnabas. He certainly enjoyed sexual congress with me, but alas, he proved no better at siring an heir."

"You killed him too," I say. "Didn't you?"

She laughs again. "Of course I did. Six months with him was all I could stand. And I'd begun to wonder if Nathaniel genuinely had died, so I hired a detective to find the gypsy hag. It took three months, but he succeeded at last and told me where I could find her. When I confronted the witch, she explained that she had falsified your death and that you lived still, though she had no idea where you had gone."

"Did you murder Barnabas before or after you found that out?" I ask.

"After, of course. I couldn't inherit the Fortescue fortune otherwise. I paid an unscrupulous solicitor to falsify the necessary documents to prove that I had found you, Nathaniel, and that we were wed in France. You were tragically lost at sea during our voyage home, which will explain your reappearance. A French frigate came upon you marooned on a sandbar, but for years, you were imprisoned as a spy."

Though she answers my questions, she keeps her gaze on Nathaniel and aims her responses at him too. Yeah, she's a total B-I-T-C-H.

"Naturally," she continues, "you sired an heir on our wedding night."

"Where's your child?" I ask.

She flattens her lips, hissing a breath out through her nostrils. "Nathaniel, darling, would you please order your *friend* to be silent?"

He squints at her with all the steely anger of a wolf. "No, I will not."

She approaches him, standing no more than an inch away when she whispers to him so softly I almost don't hear it. But I do hear, and I want to slug that woman.

"My darling," she murmurs, "there is no child—yet. We shall conceive one soon since you and I are now perfectly suited to one another, in more ways than you could imagine. Can't you smell it?"

"Smell what?" he hisses, almost as softly as she spoke.

Cordelia tilts her head to the side, exposing her throat to him. "See for yourself."

Is she trying to seduce him right in front of me? Why doesn't he tell her to go to hell? Oh wait, we're in Hell already, so he can't do that. But he could kick her ass out the door.

He doesn't.

No, instead, he leans in to sniff her neck. His eyes widen, then slide half shut, and he growls.

My stomach crashes through the floor. Well, not literally. But I do feel like a giant, metaphorical rug has been ripped out from under me and my tummy has plummeted straight through the wood planks I'm standing on. He can't want her. Can he? Not after what we did this morning in that cave. He teased me and kissed me and told me his deepest, darkest secrets.

Cordelia dresses like a proper English lady, with one of those high-collared numbers that clings to her upper body, while I'm dressed like a boy.

According to the shrew currently making time with my werewolf.

Nathaniel sniffs her neck again, this time hauling in a big lungful of whatever she smells like. He growls again, not quite as softly as before. Then he snaps straight and swivels his head to look at me. "I need to speak to Cordelia alone."

What? Oh no, he can't kick me to the curb again.

I square my shoulders and lift my chin. "I'm staying."

He rushes at me, halting a hair's breadth away. "You must leave. Cordelia and I need to have a private conversation without your interference."

Over his shoulder, I can just see Cordelia's face. And of course, she's smiling with smug satisfaction.

"I won't leave you alone with that woman," I whisper. "You can't trust her."

He glares at me for a moment, his nostrils flaring. His lips tighten, and he clamps one hand around my upper arm to drag me out the door, giving me a hard shove that forces me to stumble down the steps.

I manage to stop myself from falling down, though barely.

Nathaniel scans the crowd before his gaze settles on me again for only a second. Then he stomps back into the building.

Dozens of people are staring at me.

A man separates from the crowd, ambling up to me. "Hey, sweet thang, 'member me? I'm the one who found ya, lying there naked on the street."

"Uh, sure." I vaguely remember this guy as one of the two creeps who had poked me with their feet and calmly discussed whether I was dead.

"Way I see it," he says, "you belong to me. Finders keepers."

"Hey!" another man shouts as he pushes past other spectators to reach us. "I saw her first, ya rattlesnake. She's mine."

"Ain't no way. *I* saw her first, Arlo."

"Like hell you did, Silas. I'm taking poh-zeshin."

I guess he means "possession," but uh-uh, no way, no how, am I letting any of the creeps in this town "poh-zess" me.

The second man, Arlo, lunges for me.

When I try to hustle backward, I bump into the steps and trip, falling hard on my ass. I wince and suck in a breath as pains shoot through me.

Arlo grabs my wrist, his hand locked around it like a shackle.

I kick him in the groin.

He howls, though like a big old baby rather than a wolf. His grip on me loosens just enough that I can scramble away from him and run down the street.

The crowd swarms around me, forming a circle. I'm surrounded.

Damn, I should've grabbed that Winchester rifle before I let Nathaniel toss me out like a bag of garbage. Sure, because he so would've let me do that.

What are he and Cordelia doing in the sheriff's office?

I don't have time to worry about that. Silas and Arlo flank me, though I kind of doubt they mean to protect me. At least, not from the crowd. They face each other with me in the middle.

Silas jabs a finger toward Arlo. "I staked my claim first."

"Like hell you did," Arlo says. "I touched her first. That means I got poh-zeshin."

His buddy scoffs. "Ya kinda pushed at her with yer boot. That don't count."

"Wanna bet?" Arlo reaches inside his waistband to pull out a switchblade. He flicks it open. "Let's rassle for her."

"No way," I say. "Nobody is 'rassling' for me or 'poh-zessin' me. I belong to no one."

Silas sniggers. "Sheriff thinks you belong to him, girlie."

"He is mistaken." I glance around at the crowd, my pulse revving up when I note the looks of hungry excitement on their faces. This town really is Hell on earth, and they are the demons. Considering my situation, I alter my strategy. "Why don't we all go into the saloon and have a drink. Like friends."

"Friends?" Silas says, all but spitting the word. "Only thing I'll be doing in the saloon is taking you upstairs so's I can fuck ya private-like."

The crowd shouts their approval of his plan.

An electric tingle of fear scrapes over my skin, raising every hair. I'm surrounded. By maniacs. And I have no weapons, no way to defend myself. I once again survey the human wall around me, searching for...something.

Then I see it. A gap in the crowd. Not large, but big enough for me to slip through if I run like a hurricane wind. It's my only chance, but I need a distraction.

"I think I'll go with Arlo," I announce. "He's kind of sexy, and I'm so overdue for a ride on a bucking bronco."

Arlo puffs up. "See? She's mine."

Silas glares at the other man for a second, then he hurls his entire body at Arlo. They tumble to the ground, "rassling" like wild dogs.

And I have my opening.

I bolt through the gap in the crowd and keep running down the street, my legs pumping so hard and fast that my muscles start to scream in protest, but I keep going.

A lasso drops over me and cinches tight around my midsection. The force of my sudden stop flips my feet out from under me. I hit the ground face-first, and the impact forces all the air out of my lungs in a single explosive breath. Pain racks my body, but I can't afford to succumb to shock. With my arms pinned, I can't do more than turn over.

I roll onto my back.

Silas sneers down at me, the lasso's end grasped in his grimy hand. "Did ya think I'd let ya get away, little missy? Hell no." He points a finger at his chest. "It's gonna be me, not Arlo, who's riding you like a bronco."

No, I won't point out he's got it backwards. I'm not that dumb.

Besides, no one is riding me—today or ever. I'll die first.

Silas grasps the lasso where it's strapped to my chest and hauls me to my feet.

I try to kick him but lose my balance and almost fall down, halted by the fact Silas still grasps the lasso where it binds me. He has his hand between my breasts. The creep tugs me closer and wriggles his fingers to cop a feel of my tits. Damn, I wish I were a werewolf so I could maul this reptile.

Silas plunges his other hand into my pants pocket, feeling me up some more. "Sure are a perty one. Can't wait to ride ya."

"Give it a try, dirtbag. I'll make you regret it."

The crowd has gone silent. Too silent.

I get another tingly electric shiver of the bad kind. What's going on over there? I can't see the crowd with this creep blocking my view.

A lasso drops over Silas, cinching up so tight he gurgles. The scumbag is yanked backward, flying away from me for several feet before he whumps down. The lasso he'd used to restrain me pops out of his hand.

I wriggle out of it—and freeze when I see who captured Silas.

Nathaniel grips the end of the lasso and sears the slimeball with a molten-hot glare. The British werewolf squeezes words out between his clenched teeth. "What do you think you're doing, you slimy sack of rotting rubbish?"

Wow, he's damn hot when he gets mad. And just like that, I want to drag him back to that cave and do naughty things with him.

After he grovels for my forgiveness, of course.

CHAPTER SIXTEEN

Nathaniel

SILAS, THE SNIVELING TWAT, GAPES AT ME WITH HIS BOTTOM LIP STICK-ing out and the stench of whiskey tainting every breath that gasps out of him. I want to murder the cretin. What sort of man assaults a woman the way he has just done and threatens to violate her body? Every man in this town except for me, that's what sort.

Kylie seems shaken. Her hair and clothing are disheveled, but she stands upright with her shoulders back, so she can't be badly hurt.

Perhaps I hope she isn't, and I see what I want to see. Her predicament is entirely my fault. I should never have thrown her out of my office and left her to fend for herself, not in this town, with these wretches on the loose. Unfortunately, the sheriff's office has only two small cells for detaining miscreants.

I drop the lasso and rush over to Kylie, resisting the impulse to pull her into my arms. Letting anyone in this town see that I care for her would be dangerous and potentially fatal for her.

"Are you all right?" I murmur. "Did those fiends harm you?"

"I'm okay." She skims a hand over her left arm. "A few scrapes, that's all. Might have a bruise or two later, but I'll survive."

Kylie shouldn't need to survive. She deserves to flourish in an environment that doesn't endanger her. But I am the bastard who tossed her out of my office and left her to fend off the horde alone. Cordelia's arrival knocked me off balance, but that is no excuse for my behavior. It's an explanation, but I have no idea if Kylie will understand.

"About Cordelia," I say, then I hesitate. How can I explain this?

"You're still in love with her," Kylie says, her tone far too cavalier to be convincing. "Thank you for lending a hand with those creeps, but I can take care of myself. You're free to go back to your true love."

My what? Cordelia has never been any sort of love to me. I'd admired her beauty and lusted for her, but I hardly know the woman. I want—need to discuss this with Kylie, but I can't do that out here on the street.

"Come with me, please," I whisper. "I will explain everything once we're inside the sheriff's office. It's not safe out here."

She twists her lips into a strange expression and studies me for a moment that feels like an hour. "Fine, I'll go with you. But I'm still pissed." She thumps her fist on my chest. "At you, Sheriff Asshat."

Bloody hell. She's calling me an "asshat" again. I assume "pissed" means she's angry since it sounds similar to "pissy," the word she used when she was annoyed with me. Evidently, it doesn't mean she wants to urinate on me.

"Shouldn't you be angry with Silas and Arlo?" I ask.

"Oh, I'm pissed at them too." She thumps my chest again. "But you're the one who hur—Well, you know what you did."

She seems vaguely embarrassed, though I can't decipher why. Might "hur" have meant "hurt"? Perhaps she failed to finish the word.

I have hurt her, haven't I? Again and again.

"We must go," I say as I turn and head for the sheriff's office.

Kylie follows me inside and leans against the desk with her arse resting on its edge. She crosses her arms over her chest, though she slouches a touch.

I peer out the window. The crowd is dispersing now that the uproar has ended. Silas and Arlo are walking into the saloon.

And I want to rush over there to beat them into bloody pulps.

Though I turn toward Kylie, I maintain a discreet distance between us.

She glances around, her brows rising. "Where's dear sweet Cordelia?"

I point toward the door that leads to the jail cells. "In there. I've confined her."

Kylie straightens, leaning forward. Her expression brightens. "You locked her up? In a cell? I bet she's livid."

"Yes." I shuffle closer to her. "I don't care if Cordelia is angry. I don't care about her at all."

"Uh-*huh*. I guess you were sniffing her strictly to find out if she uses deodorant."

Deodorant? I have heard the word once or twice, and I believe I understand what Kylie means when she uses that term. "I sniffed her because I needed to know for certain what she is."

"Uh-huh."

"I do not want Cordelia. I've met her on three occasions, all of which were brief. I do not know her, nor do I want to."

Kylie rolls her eyes. "Sure, that's why you were growling and fisting your hands and leaning in close enough you could've kissed her."

She's jealous. I'm not imagining that. And once again, I've hurt her.

I move closer, closing my hands around her upper arms. "Cordelia is a vile creature. More than that, though, she is a wolf."

"Yeah, she looks like the man-eater type. I get why you're hot for her. Men like to be abused by bad girls."

How on earth can I convince her I do not want Cordelia Atherton? My former fiancée must believe she's Lady Wilderhampton now, based on her two fatal marriages, but neither of my uncles legally inherited the title since I am still alive. I won't call her Lady Wilderhampton, that's for certain, and Mrs. Fortescue sounds odd.

"I've told you about my past," I say to Kylie. "How can you believe I want to be abused by anyone?"

She bows her head and shrugs. "Cordelia has some kind of hold on you."

"Yes, but not the way you're suggesting." I hook a finger under her chin, compelling her to look at me. "She is a wolf. Cordelia has become like me."

"She's a werewolf?"

"Yes. That is what I smelled on her. I feel no desire for Cordelia."

Kylie chews on her bottom lip. "I don't get it. How did Cordelia become a wolf? Did the gypsy curse her too?"

"I cannot explain that, and I was about to ask her when I heard the commotion outside." I scratch my jaw as I consider how Kylie will react to another aspect of my former fiancée, but I feel I must tell her. "I smelled something else when I sniffed Cordelia. Something dark and pungent, not at all like the scent of a wolf or a human. I can't identify the odor, but it made me...uneasy."

"Is that the British way of saying you chucked me out into the street because of what she smelled like?"

"Yes." I take a step back and offer her my hand. "Come. Let's interrogate Cordelia together."

"Seriously? You want me there, intruding on your personal stuff."

"This is not personal. Cordelia means nothing to me."

"You're a very confusing man. Do you know that?"

"Yes, I am well aware of the fact that I'm a bleeding arsehole. Now, may we go speak with Cordelia?"

Kylie slips her hand into mine, and we go through the closed door which leads into the hallway that houses the two jail cells. One is empty. In the other, Cordelia sits on a Spartan cot, ramrod straight, chin held high. Yes, she is always the regal lady—except when she begged me to ravish her on that night so many years ago. Perhaps she has never been as much of a lady as I'd assumed. She certainly harbors darkness inside her, and I'm referring to more than the wolf within.

I keep hold of Kylie's hand when we stop in front of Cordelia's cell. "We want answers. You will give them, or I will keep you confined here for the rest of your natural life. How did you become a wolf?"

Cordelia glances at my hand, the one clasped around Kylie's, and her lips pucker briefly. Then she aims her sweetest smile at me, the one that used to fool me but does not any longer. "I was devastated when you vanished. Can't you see that, darling? I wanted to be reunited with you at any cost."

"I am not that easily fooled, Cordelia. You've already confessed that all you cared about was getting your greedy little hands on the Fortescue fortune."

"Yes, I wanted the money. But I did love you, Nathaniel, so very much."

Perhaps I might believe her if she weren't fluttering her eyelashes at me and speaking in a tone dripping with false sweetness. The woman has no scruples whatsoever and, I suspect, no conscience either.

"The truth," I demand. "Now."

"Better tell him," Kylie says. "He's one badass werewolf, and you won't last long if he gets mad at you."

I resist the urge to glance at Kylie, despite the fact her use of the word "badass" has me flummoxed. If "asshat" means I'm an arse, then "badass" must mean I'm a rotten arse. Or something of that nature. Her tone, however, implied she was complimenting me.

Twenty-first century Americans are even more baffling than the ones in this time.

"Nathaniel, darling," Cordelia says, "would you please instruct your servant not to speak to me?"

"No, I will not. And stop calling me 'darling,' or I will rip your throat out." I lean in and growl at her. "Answer *now*."

"My, you've grown tiresome over the past five years." Cordelia sighs and approaches the bars. "After I discovered what that gypsy had done to you, I realized how powerful I could be if I became a wolf too. No man would dare try to control me when I have the supernatural strength of a cursed beast simmering inside me. So I paid that gypsy witch an enormous amount of money to give me the same curse she laid down on you."

"I don't believe you. The Rom woman wouldn't do that, not for you."

Cordelia smirks. "Well, perhaps she needed a slight inducement. I poisoned her daughter and wouldn't give her the antidote until after she made me a wolf."

"Damn," Kylie says. "You are one stone-cold evil bitch."

"I'd rather be evil and rich than righteous and poor." She grasps the cell bars and slides her hands up and down them in an almost sensual manner. "So you see, Nathaniel, we belong together. You can't be with a normal woman. You need a wolf like me to feed your animal hunger." She throws a haughty glance at Kylie. "If you try to mate with this child, you might kill her. She's not as strong as you or I."

But I've already "mated" with Kylie, and she did not die.

Cordelia seems enormously pleased with herself, though I can't deduce why. She pushes her face between the bars as far as she can, then drags her tongue across her lips. "You've already had her, haven't you? I imagine the gypsy never told you what happens when a wolf mates with a human. If she doesn't die during pregnancy or childbirth, the babe will be a deformed monster."

She must be lying. Cordelia cannot know any of that, despite what she implied the gypsy told her. I used to think Cordelia Atherton was an angel, but now I see she has always been a demon, even before she became a wolf.

I have wasted enough time listening to Cordelia's rubbish. But I need to know one more thing before I leave her to rot in her cell. "How did you arrive in the Outlands?"

She laughs. "Honestly, Nathaniel, you've grown even stupider since last we met. You of all people ought to know how anyone gains entry into this region." She runs her hands up and down the bars again in the same sensual manner as before. "Once I became a wolf, I experienced a strong urge to find a home. So I followed the call and wound up here."

Kylie studies Cordelia, her jaw tight and her gaze never wavering. "Only the worst people wind up here. I guess murdering two husbands earned you a one-way ticket to Hell on earth."

"And how did you end up in this place, dear?" Cordelia asks. "What terrible thing have you done?"

Nothing, that's what Kylie has done. The medallion must have sent her here, though I can't comprehend why.

Cordelia returns her attention to me. "Fate brought us together again, and you cannot fight the hand of destiny. You belong with me, not your little pet. We can hunt together under the full moon and mate like the animals we are. This is your fate, Nathaniel, and you know it."

The wolf in me is rousing, but not for the reasons she wants. My inner beast wants to tear Cordelia to shreds so that she might never harm Kylie.

The evil bitch, as Kylie called her, snakes an arm between the bars to reach out to me. "Be with me, Nathaniel, where you belong. Then tonight, when the moon is full, we can feast on her flesh."

Hot fury scorches through me like a torch dropped into a pool of kerosene. I can't control the inferno even if I wanted to, not when Cordelia has threatened Kylie. I seize Cordelia's arm and yank it, slamming her entire body into the bars.

Her eyes widen, and a gasp bursts out of her.

I slant in until my face is a hair's breadth from hers. "Never threaten Kylie again. If you so much as glance at her, I will rip your desiccated heart from your chest and devour it."

Kylie lays a hand on my forearm. "Relax, Nathaniel. She's locked up where she can't hurt anyone. Let's just leave her in there to stew for a while, huh? We have other things to do."

Other things. Yes, I'd promised to teach her how to shoot a rifle so she can witness my transformation tonight. But now, I wonder if that's wise. Perhaps I should lock her in my bedroom where even I can't get to her.

"You are correct," I say. "We should leave Cordelia here."

I clasp Kylie's hand, feeling more at ease with her warm skin on mine, and lead her out of the building. I have one task to accomplish now.

Convince Kylie to stay in my bedroom tonight.

CHAPTER SEVENTEEN

Kylie

NATHANIEL TAKES ME BACK TO THE SALOON AND OUR LITTLE ROOM upstairs. Okay, maybe I should worry that I've started to think of it as "our" room, but that doesn't bother me. I should probably be more concerned about why Nathaniel means so much to me when I've known him for less than twenty-four hours, but that also doesn't bother me. Sometimes he growls, and sometimes he behaves like a total jerk. But I know he does that only because he's afraid.

Of what? Hurting me, for sure, and possibly whatever he smelled on Cordelia.

He wouldn't hurt me on purpose, not physically. He snarled all that nasty stuff at me earlier because he thinks he needs to protect me from himself. Somehow, deep down and in a way I don't understand, I know he would never attack me, not even when he's a full-on wolf.

Yeah, I've probably gone insane.

But I don't care about that either.

Nathaniel shuts the door to our room and leans back against it. He seems haggard now, like his confrontation with Cordelia has left him drained.

I want to hug him, but I decide it's best if I sit on the bed and wait for him to speak. Unless I get sick and tired of waiting.

He rubs his eyes and groans.

"What's wrong?" I ask. Sure, I only lasted a few seconds before I stopped waiting for him to speak. Can anyone blame me? An already bizarre situation has gotten even weirder.

Nathaniel rests his head on the door, staring up at the ceiling. "My ex-fiancée is here in the Outlands, and she has become a wolf. Is it incomprehensible that I might need a few moments to digest that information?"

"Fine. You digest away. I'll figure out how to shoot a rifle on my own."

I stand up.

Nathaniel leaps across the space between us and drags me into his body, his strong hands fastened around my arms like vises. "You cannot leave this room. Tonight, the moon will be—"

"Full. Yeah, I heard you every other time you said that." I wriggle, trying to get free, but I all accomplish is to make him growl softly. "Let go of me, you big old alpha jerk."

"Not until you vow to remain here until morning."

"You said you'd let me go with you tonight."

"The situation has changed."

I feel his dick getting stiffer and bigger, and I can't stop my body from tingling in every way that I don't want it to right now. "Are you planning to have a wild night of wolf sex with Cordelia?"

"I would rather shag a cactus than lay one finger on Cordelia."

"Well, if she's staying locked up, you have no reason not to let me go with you tonight."

"I am a beast, Kylie." He lashes his arms around me. His mouth hovers millimeters from mine. "I could injure you without meaning to do it. Once the full moon rises, the wolf within takes control and I transform. The danger is too great. I should never have suggested you could accompany me tonight."

Jeez, I get that he's freaked by the mysterious appearance of his ex-fiancée, but I am not some prissy girl who faints at the sight of blood. And I know he will never hurt me. I want to witness his transformation, for reasons I can't explain. I *need* to see it. Since he won't give up on the idea that it's too dangerous for me to go with him, I have only one card left to play.

"What about Arlo and Silas?" I ask. "They both want to get their hands on me. And I bet they're royally ticked at you for stopping them from taking what they want. What if they try to get me while I'm locked inside this room?"

"They can't. This entire room is fortified with cast iron, and there is only one key to the lock."

"Which I have."

I gaze into his eyes, transfixed by their gleaming black centers and the gray irises that seem to shimmer like liquid silver. But a memory blasts through my mind, shattering the spell. I remember Silas shoving his greasy paw into my pants pocket and groping me. Had that been all he'd done? His fingers had moved around like he was searching for something. I'd forgotten about that once Nathaniel lassoed the dirtbag and hauled me back to the sheriff's office.

I struggle to reach into my pocket, which isn't easy when Nathaniel has me mashed to his body. My fingers find...

Oh shit.

"Uh, there's a problem," I say, then I wince. "Silas stole the room key from my pocket. Neither of us can lock me in."

His face goes blank for a second. Then he mutters under his breath, "Bollocks."

"I'm sorry, but it's not my fault. You kicked me out of your office."

"Which I did only because you insist upon vexing me." He grasps the doorknob while still holding onto me. "I will locate Silas and retrieve the key."

"And you think he'll just hand it over."

He grumbles, but it doesn't sound like words.

"Let me try," I say. "Maybe Silas will give it to me if I pretend to—"

"No," he barks, though not in a doggy way. "I will remedy the situation."

He throws me over his shoulder and marches downstairs, where he pauses at the bar. "Lucy, have you seen Silas?"

"No, yer lordyship. Sorry."

He stomps outside and down the porch steps, then he sets me on my feet and clamps his hand around mine. "We will find Silas."

Nathaniel half drags me down the street. We check every building, and he snarls questions at every person we meet, but we don't find Silas. If he's in town, he must've found a place to hide that Nathaniel doesn't know about. When he starts heading toward the narrow path that leads away from town, I kick him in the shin. Hard.

And he finally stops to look at me.

"We can't search the whole desert," I say. "Unless you can sniff out Silas with your wolf nose."

"I cannot, since I have no idea in which direction to search."

"So what was your plan? Traipse around the desert hoping you'll catch his scent?"

He grinds his teeth, his jaw working.

"Oh come on," I say. "That *was* your plan? Give it up, Nathaniel. The creep got away, for now. And I am starving, so maybe you should feed me instead of dragging me all over creation."

He scrubs a hand over his face. "Damnation."

Thankfully, he escorts me back to our mini fortress above the saloon, and then he goes back downstairs to get our food. The wolfman ordered me to stay in the room. I do that, but not because he ordered me to do it. I could use a bit of alone time.

When Nathaniel returns, he's carrying a tray loaded up with what looks like typical Old West food, assuming John Wayne movies provided accurate info about that. We wind up eating beans, tough biscuits, some kind of dried-out meat similar to jerky, hard cheese, and dried fruit. He also brought coffee. This morning, he'd brought me pretty much the same food, minus the cheese and fruit.

He sits in the chair beside the bed and props his feet on the mattress while still holding the tray of food.

I settle my butt on his lap.

"What are you doing?" he asks, seeming suspicious.

"What do you think I'm doing? Sitting on your lap. I want to eat *with* you, not somewhere in the vicinity of you."

"Why?"

"So we can feed each other."

"I'm quite capable of feeding myself."

"That's not the point." I take the tray from him and place it on my lap. "Feeding each other is fun. Come on, don't get grumpy about it. Give it a try."

He eyes me sideways, his lips contorted. "If you insist."

I'm guessing Nathaniel has never done this before. He's had sex with plenty of women, based on what I read between the lines when he told me about his life after his father announced he would inherit the family fortune. But he'd also mentioned, when he told me the story of how he became a wolf, that most of the women he'd slept with were prostitutes.

The point is, he needs to have some fun.

I pick up a piece of cheese and move it toward his mouth while making choo-choo noises. "Open up, Nathaniel. Let the food train pull into the station. That's your mouth, in case you were confused."

He scrunches up his entire face.

So I imitate a train whistle while I touch the cheese to his lips. "Choo-choo, Nathaniel. Open up, or I'll tickle you."

He grudgingly opens his mouth—about half an inch.

I break off a small piece of cheese and shove it between his lips. "Chew it all up."

Once he's chewed and swallowed, I offer him a piece of jerky.

He clamps his mouth shut, but he's smirking instead of looking annoyed.

I do the choo-choo thing again, but this time, he refuses to open his mouth. "You know what I'll have to do if you don't take this bite."

His smirk deepens.

Does he want me to tickle him? Is he being playful? Yeah, I think he is. The realization makes me so giddy that for a couple of seconds, I can't move. Then I set the jerky back on the plate and tickle his belly until he's laughing so hard his eyes swater.

"Had enough?" I ask, holding the jerky near his mouth again. "Are you ready to surrender?"

"Not quite yet."

"Guess I need to up the ante."

I pull his shirt out of his pants and lift it to reveal his impressive abs, then I press my mouth to his belly and blow, making my lips vibrate.

He laughs even harder this time.

God, he's sexier than ever when he does that. He seems younger when he's smiling and laughing instead of scowling and growling.

He grabs the piece of jerky and eats it.

Before I can take any food for myself, he grabs a chunk of cheese and feeds it to me. We spend the rest of our meal doing that, taking turns slipping pieces of food into each other's mouths while tickling each other in between bites. Once we're done eating, Nathaniel sets the tray on the bedside table and loops his arms around my waist, latching his hands at my hip.

"Feel better now that I've fed you?" he asks.

"Yes. Thank you." I gaze at the empty plate, remembering all the twenty-first-century meals I'd eaten. "Cowboy food hit the spot, but I'd kill for some buffalo wings."

"Buffalo do not have wings. They aren't birds."

I clamp my teeth over my lips until the need to laugh subsides. "A buffalo wing is a chicken wing that's fried and smothered in spicy sauce."

He looks so adorably confused that I want to kiss him. But I don't get the chance.

"I will secure you in a jail cell tonight," he says. "I would feel much less worried for your well-being if I know you're inside a relatively safe structure."

"You want me to hang out with my new best friend Cordelia?"

He throws his head back and shuts his eyes. "Bloody hell. I forgot about her."

Maybe I shouldn't feel smug about that fact, but I kind of do.

"Tell me one thing," I say. "How did you create this iron-clad room? I can't imagine how you got all the iron here when nobody can enter the Outlands unless they've done something bad."

Maybe everybody else in this town belongs here, but I do not believe Nathaniel did anything so awful that he deserves to be consigned to this place. He believes it, I'm sure.

"I did not create this room," he says. "It was here when I arrived, almost as if it were waiting for me. Lucy gave me the key, but she knew nothing about the room itself. I do not know why it was built."

"Weird. Now, about locking me up with my bestie Cordelia..."

He rubs his forehead and sighs. "Perhaps you should come with me tonight."

CHAPTER EIGHTEEN

Nathaniel

I CANNOT EXPLAIN WHY I SAID THAT. TAKE HER WITH ME TOnight? It's madness. Once the moon rises, I will become a beast in the truest sense of the word. She won't be safer with me than she would be in a jail cell. What if I kill her while I'm out of my mind and in wolf form? Yet if Silas does have a key to this room, she won't be safe here either.

Damn and blast. What am I meant to do?

"So, I can go with you?" Kylie asks. "That's what you kind of implied."

"That is what I meant, but I still feel it's too dangerous. Leaving you here might be equally treacherous. Perhaps a cell is the safest option."

"But if you're turning into a wolf tonight, and Cordelia is cursed too, doesn't that mean she'll transform during the full moon? What if she breaks out of her cell? I'll be right there, fast food for a werewolf."

I groan and bow my head. She's right, of course, and I'm a blooming moron.

Kylie crooks a finger under my chin, lifting until I can't refuse to look at her anymore. "Let's go back to Plan A. You teach me how to use a rifle, and I go with you tonight."

"All right."

She kisses the tip of my nose. "Thank you."

I grunt. What else can I do? Neither plan seems adequate to protect her, so I've been forced to let her choose which one we implement.

Kylie bites one side of her bottom lip. "Do you, um, turn into a wolf every night or only when the moon is full? I wondered because you went out last night, and I heard a wolf howling. But that wasn't the full moon."

"It was nearly full. I can become a wolf at any time, day or night, but the call is strongest on the night of the full moon and the nights before and after that."

"Do you kill animals and eat them?"

"Yes, but it's the blood I crave, not the meat." I cannot believe I'm discussing this with her. No one else has ever asked me for details about my nocturnal activities.

"Blood?" she says. "I thought you were a werewolf, not a vampire."

"I do not sink my fangs into the veins of living creatures in order to feed. I rip flesh apart to lick up the, ah, blood. The creatures on which I feed generally die, but it's not a swift or clean death, as far as I know."

"You rip them apart?" She wrinkles her nose. "That's disgusting."

When I start to speak, she pinches my lips together with her thumb and forefinger.

I could force her to relinquish my lips, but I seem to lose the ability to move whenever she's this close to me.

"Wait a minute," she says, then she releases my mouth. "You said you don't remember anything that happens after you transform."

"Yes, that is true."

"Then how do you know you've killed any living things? You were wrong about Cordelia."

"I wake up covered in blood."

"Okay, that does sound suspiciously fatal." She taps a finger on her mouth as if she's thinking. "But do you mean literally covered in blood, like from head to toe? Or do you mean there's blood in several places but not all over you?"

I need to consider her questions for a moment because I have never bothered to think about that before. When I awaken after a night as a wolf, I see the blood, but only for the briefest moment. Then I rush to cleanse myself of it. Am I truly covered in blood in the morning? I search my mind for the answer.

"Not head to toe," I finally tell her. "I suppose you could say I'm spattered with blood."

"Spattered? That leaves plenty of doubts about whether you kill anything. Maybe you injure animals, but they survive and recover."

"You insist on believing the best of me, but I can't figure out why."

"Because you're a good man, underneath all that snarling and growling and saying nasty things to make me go away."

"I am sorry for the way I've behaved."

"Yeah, I know. It's okay." She brushes her fingers through my hair. "You were scared, and that's the only reason why you acted like such a jerk after our cave interlude."

Why this woman forgives me and believes in me, I cannot fathom. She should find a normal, even-tempered man who is capable of giving her the sort of life she deserves.

But I can't give her up. I *need* her.

Yes, I am a selfish bastard.

Kylie sweeps her gaze around the room, surveying every inch of it including the ceiling before she looks at me again. "I'm still confused about one thing. Why don't you stay in this room every night instead of going outside? You couldn't hurt any creature if you were locked in here."

"I've tried that. You can see the result." I gesture toward the floor and the walls. "I gouged those marks into the wood. The wolf in me desperately needs to run free. After the transformation, I tried to escape from this room but couldn't. I awakened feeling starved and in a truly black mood, not to mention bruised, bloody, and missing all my fingernails and toenails."

"Ouch. How many times did you lock yourself in here?"

"Twice. After the second time, I was in such a state that I nearly assaulted a man because he made a sarcastic comment about my physical appearance." I shift uncomfortably in my chair, despite having Kylie perched on my lap. "I decided it was safer for my sanity and the townsfolk's well-being if I escaped into the wilds at night."

"But you said you can become a wolf anytime, not just during the full moon."

"Yes, but I prefer not to do it." I slap her arse. "Come, let me teach you how to use a Winchester '73 model repeating rifle. You may need it tonight."

"I'm ready to follow your instructions, my lord."

"Only servants call an earl 'my lord.' You are not in my employ." Though I do enjoy hearing her call me that. It makes me want to ravish her right here in this chair.

"I was being sarcastic, Nathaniel."

"Yes, I am aware of that." I stand up, with her in my arms, and set her feet on the floor. "It's time for your training."

We retrieve the rifle from the sheriff's office, and I take a moment to ensure Cordelia is still trapped in her cell. She is, but I have no idea if a jail cell will contain her once the moon rises. Kylie is beside me while I contemplate the strength of the bars, and Cordelia watches us with a look of self-satisfaction on her face. Does she know something I haven't discovered yet? Can she escape this cell?

I have no other options. All I can do is pray the cell will contain her.

Kylie and I leave the sheriff's office and head to a spot behind the blacksmith's shop so I can teach her how to use the Winchester rifle. She learns quickly, and her aim improves with every shot until I can't help marveling at her skill. I had needed more than a few hours to become proficient with any sort of firearm. Of course, she did mention she had experience with carnival shooting galleries.

"You are the cleverest woman I've ever met," I tell her after she fires her last round of our practice session. Her shot hits the center of the target, and I can't help smiling at her. "You learn faster than anyone I've ever encountered. I'm impressed."

"Thanks." She grins. "Guess shooting fake ducks was my prep for meeting a hot werewolf."

"What does 'hot' mean to you?"

"That you are gorgeous and irresistible, and I'd love to get naked with you again."

I want that too, but I won't do it. "What happens tonight will not be hot."

"You don't know what it will be like." She's holding the rifle at her side, aimed at the ground, but now she raps its barrel against her thigh. "I've got this, which means I can handle whatever happens."

The sun is setting, and the moon will rise very soon, so we begin our journey out of town and into the desert.

As we pass the livery stable, Kylie asks, "Can't we get there faster on horseback?"

"Yes, but horses are terrified of werewolves."

"Guess we walk, then. How far do we need to go?"

I slip my hand into hers while we take our first steps beyond the cluster of buildings. "The butte is the safest location since it's away from town and no one else goes there."

"You mean it's your favorite spot for wolfing out on the down-low."

"Perhaps I would agree with that statement if I understood it."

"I meant it's where you like to go when you're about to 'transform' into a wolf because it's your secret place where nobody will see you."

"Correct." I must be growing accustomed to her strange manner of speaking. It no longer irritates me.

The sun sinks below the horizon, and darkness creeps over the world little by little. The night creatures awaken, their sounds growing louder and more widespread as we continue our journey toward the dark mound of the butte. Soon, the first stars emerge. By the time we halt at the base of the butte, the moon has slid above the horizon on its journey toward its zenith. We haven't long now until the call will trigger my transformation.

The brilliant glow of the full moon illuminates our surroundings.

"Aren't we going inside?" Kylie asks. "To your secret wolfie cavern?"

"No. I need to be outdoors when I feel the moon's call." I bow my head and scratch the back of my neck, unable to look at Kylie for reasons I cannot understand. "Now I need to, ah, remove my clothing."

She laughs, though the sound is soft and gentle. "I've seen you buck naked already. Your nudity tonight won't shock me."

No, she won't be shocked. I suppose I'm feeling uncomfortable with the idea of Kylie watching me transform.

"Hey, are there normal wolves around here?" she asks. "Should I be watching out for them?"

"There are wolves in the Utah Territory, but not in the Outlands."

"Guess it's too spooky here for them, huh?"

"Could we not speak? I feel odd about this."

She cradles my face in her hands and kisses me sweetly. "You're embarrassed, aren't you? Relax, I won't panic when I see you go all wolfman. And I won't be disgusted either, though I'm sure you won't believe that until I prove it."

"Perhaps I am a bit unnerved by the prospect of you witnessing the change. I'm also concerned for your safety."

"Don't worry about me." She raises the rifle. "I'm a crack shot, remember?"

I close my eyes and issue a silent prayer that she's right. Then I peel off my clothing. The moon has just reached its zenith, and the call pulls at me. My breathing grows labored. I glance at Kylie one last time, and when I speak, my voice has become rough and infused with a growling undertone.

"Move away," I tell her. "It is about to begin."

She takes a few steps backward.

A gust of wind swirls around us, tousling her hair, and it carries with it the faintest scent. I sniff the air but can't ascertain what I smell. The call tugs at me with more strength, stripping away the vestiges of my rational mind and erasing all thoughts.

The beast is about to rise.

CHAPTER NINETEEN

Kylie

NATHANIEL IS BUCK NAKED. I LOVE OGLING HIS BODY, BUT THE LOOK on his face makes me anxious. His eyes are wild, his mouth is open, and he has started to growl softly, low in his throat. He won't attack me. I believe that for no good reason at all, but reason has no place in the Outlands. This is a world of magic and danger.

But Nathaniel will not hurt me. The danger comes from other sources.

His entire body jerks, and he squeezes his eyes shut so tightly it contorts his whole face. He cries out, then crashes down onto the ground flat on his face. For a moment, he just lies there, immobilized.

I grasp the rifle with both hands, aiming the muzzle at the ground. I've got fifteen rounds in the magazine. Nathaniel wanted me to keep more bullets in my pocket, but if I need more than fifteen, I doubt I'll get a chance to reload.

His fingers twitch. Then his head jerks. Finally, his body shudders from head to toe. Inch by inch, he pushes up with his arms, rising onto all fours with his head down.

My pulse thunders in my ears, my heart beating so fast that I start to feel weak. *Breathe, dummy.* Yeah, passing out right now seems like a surefire way to become food for the wolf. *If* he kills after the transformation. I'm still not convinced he does. But I can't help feeling a mixture of fear and excitement. Every fine hair on my body shivers and stiffens in anticipation of whatever might come next.

His body contorts as his bones crack and his spine deforms.

And he screams.

The cry echoes off the butte and reverberates through the night, triggering a fierce shiver that makes my teeth clack together. I take a couple of slow, deep breaths and widen my stance while maintaining my hold on the rifle with both hands. I wanted to witness this. Fear is natural, but I can't let my anxiety take control.

I'll stay strong—for him.

While I watch in stunned silence, standing here glued in place, Nathaniel's body transforms. He wasn't using that word as a metaphor. No, his basic structure, from his muscles to his skeleton, seems to disintegrate beneath his skin and reshape itself. His body shrinks and almost melts, becoming a blurry mess that my brain can't interpret as anything other than...a supernatural shift. My God, he's shapeshifting right before my eyes. More screams are torn from his throat, but they gradually transmute into animalistic sounds. Grunts, growls, and finally...

A howl pierces the night, the sound so close that I wince as it vibrates my eardrums.

The blurry mass solidifies into a large gray wolf.

I gape at the animal. That's Nathaniel Fortescue. He became a wolf in the most literal sense. I guess I hadn't fully accepted the idea, not on a conscious level, until this moment. He's not a wolf-like man. He is a genuine wolf.

Holy shit.

I glance down at the rifle in my hands. Suddenly, I know beyond any doubt that I don't need this weapon. Not for him. The gorgeous gray wolf in front of me would never hurt me.

So I kneel on the ground and lay the rifle down.

The wolf gazes at me steadily, tipping his head to the side.

"Hey there," I say, holding out my hand to him, palm up. "I won't hurt you. Come over here, Nathaniel."

When I say his name, the wolf's head pops up, his ears pricked.

"That's right," I tell him. "I know you're Nathaniel, so come closer. Please."

The wolf pads over to me and sniffs my palm. I giggle a little when his whiskers tickle my skin. He licks my palm. I raise my other hand to scratch behind his ears, which makes him close his eyes halfway and turn his head to the side like he loves this.

I'm scratching the ears of the man I had sex with this morning. The furry beast in front of me is Nathaniel Fortescue. Maybe I still can't quite wrap my head around that fact.

He lies down, rolling over onto his back.

Doe he actually want me to rub his belly? What the hell. My life can't get much weirder, so I rub his belly with my palm. His eyes drift half-closed again, and I swear he's smiling.

If Nathaniel doesn't remember this in the morning, I might remind him just to see the horrified look on his face. Or maybe he won't be horrified. Maybe he'll beg me to rub his tummy and scratch behind his ears.

The wolf jumps up and nudges my hip, then looks up at me.

Does he want something? If so, I've got no clue what it is.

He nudges my hip again, with more vigor, and a hard object pokes me.

The medallion. It's still in my pocket. Does he want me to take it out? I don't know why he would, but I see no reason not to do it. I dig the medallion out and hold it between my thumb and forefinger. "Did you want this?"

Wolf Nathaniel nods once.

I hold the medallion out to him, cradled in my palm. "Here you go."

He shakes his head, then bumps his nose into my hand.

"Sorry, sweetie, but I have no idea what you want me to do."

The wolf touches his nose to the medallion and looks at me again with that steady gaze.

Awareness shivers through me, and suddenly, I know what he wants. Got no clue how I know, but I do. To hell with logic. I take hold of the hemp cord the medallion hangs from and drape it around my neck. The disk itself hangs down my chest, and I tuck it inside my shirt, between my breasts.

Soothing warmth emanates from the medallion, and my skin tingles. It's not fear, though. The sensation spreads over my skin, spurring my nipples to harden, and sweeps even lower to gather between my thighs where I'm growing wetter every second. I suck in a sharp breath, overwhelmed by the power of what I'm feeling.

The wolf backs away from me several paces.

His form blurs and shimmers, then a flash of white light blinds me. I instinctively raise an arm to shield my eyes. When the brilliance fades, I dare to peek over my arm.

Nathaniel stands there. Naked. Aroused. Breathing hard. He glances around, his brows crinkled, until his focus lands on me. "What happened? Did I not transform? It isn't morning yet."

I approach him, stopping an arm's length away. "You turned into a wolf. I saw it happen. Then you kind of asked me to get out the medallion."

"Asked? If I was a wolf, I couldn't speak. Could I?"

He seems confused, and I'm right there with him. "No, you howled once. Then you sniffed my hand. But when I hung the medallion around my neck, something happened. I got tingly all over and then you reverted to being a man."

"Yes, I can see that."

"It didn't take as long as the first transformation. You just kind of blurred and poofed into being human again."

He's still breathing harder than usual, and his erection waves between us. He glances down at it. "No, I can't—This isn't right."

"What isn't right? You're seriously turned on, but since you're human again, that means we can...you know...do it."

His head jerks up, and his eyes widen. "No, we can't. Though I might be in human form again, I still feel like a wolf. But my hunger for flesh has become a hunger for something else."

The way he's staring at my body and licking his lips, I understand what that "something else" is. And I'm totally on board for that.

I lay my hands on his naked chest. "Relax, I'm not afraid. You won't hurt me, and I want you so damn much right now that it's kind of embarrassing. Please, I need this."

"But I—I'm still behaving like an animal. This won't be like the first time." His breathing has grown heavier again, his chest heaving, and his voice is rougher. "You have no idea what you're asking me to do."

"I can handle it."

He shakes his head slowly, his lips parted and his cheeks ruddy.

Okay, it's up to me to make the first move.

So I whip my shirt off over my head, kick off my boots, tear my socks off, and wriggle out of my pants.

He shakes his head with more vehemence this time, and his voice has become a growl. "You shouldn't have done that, Kylie. I—can't—stop—"

Nathaniel grasps my waist and flips me around, then he wraps his arms around my midsection and hugs me to his hard, hot, aroused body. His erection feels as hard as steel against my back. Oh God, this is happening. I'm about to let a ravenous werewolf mate with me under the full moon, out in the open.

And I've never wanted anything more.

He drops to his knees, forcing me to kneel with him. His breaths bluster out of him and flutter my hair, but it's the steel-hard erection pinned between our bodies that has me fighting for every ounce of air.

I can't think with my heart beating so fast, but I know one thing for sure. I've been waiting for this moment since the first time I laid eyes on him. Though I hadn't consciously known who or what he was, somehow, deep in my soul, I always knew.

Nathaniel shoves his nose against my neck and sniffs my skin several times, then he growls, though it's not a menacing sound. No, it's almost sensual, and my body reacts by getting wetter and achier. The liquid dribbling down my inner thighs testifies to how much I want this, want him, no matter what he is or might become. I raise my arms to grasp the back of his neck. He sniffs and licks my throat while his hands wander down my thighs, pushing between them until his fingers touch the slickness there.

He lifts a hand to his mouth, his nostrils flaring as he takes in the scent of my cream, then he shoves his fingers into his mouth and sucks on them. His eyes shut for a heart-beat. He groans with such deep satisfaction that it reso-nates through his chest and into me. Sharp growly noises grunt out of him as he clamps his free hand around my breast, and with the hand still lodged between my thighs, he begins to rub my clitoris. He's not gentle about it, but I don't care. He gives my tit a rough squeeze, then whisks that hand over my skin, up and down, side to side, like he's fondling me the wolfie way.

That finger between my thighs moves faster, scraping my flesh, pumping up the pressure inside me until I'm whim-pering and begging him to make me come. My body feels like it's electrified, as if the power source throbs deep with-in my sex.

Nathaniel shifts his hips, pushing his hard cock between my legs and rubbing it along my cleft.

Every muscle inside me tightens, forcing my body to bow inward. The intensity of the impending orgasm robs me of breath, of thought, of anything resembling common sense, and I come so hard I scream, the cry echoing around us. My inner muscles clench at nothing, and he keeps rubbing his erection between my legs, refusing to stop until I'm completely spent.

I sag against him, gasping for breath. Little by little, my heartbeat slows and I regain the ability to breathe. For a moment, Nathaniel just holds me. He smooths damp hair away from my eyes and nuzzles my cheek. His tenderness astounds me, considering the state he's in—wildly aroused and half-beast.

He lashes an arm around my waist and shoves his free hand between our bodies, flattening his palm on my back and pushing until I drop onto all fours. I spread my legs for him, which makes him growl again.

Then he grasps my hips and thrusts into me.

I gasp at the sudden sensation of fullness, of him inside me buried to the hilt. This feels different but no less incred-ible than the first time when we'd looked each other in the eye the entire time. I can't see him now, but I hear his rough breathing and feel his cock inside me and his balls brushing my ass. He bends over me to plant his hands on the ground alongside me, so that now his body cages mine.

And he thrusts again. And again.

He goes slow at first, like some part of him realizes he needs to give me time to get used to this before he lets go. My fingers dig into the earth, and my body rocks with every lunge of his hips. I know, though I can't explain how, that he needs to fuck me like a wild animal despite the way he's holding back right now.

"Go for it," I tell him. "Don't hold back. Take me any way you need to."

Nathaniel throws his head back and howls, then he bends over me to plant his hands on the ground at either side of my body. He starts pounding into me with such strength that my knees scrape across the earth and my breasts bounce beneath me. I cry out several times until the mounting pressure inside me steals my breath completely and all I can do is grit my teeth and wait for the climax to consume me. Hotter, harder, the need escalates like a star about to go supernova. He clenches a handful of my hair in his fist and yanks my head back, growling fiercely.

And he clamps his teeth onto my neck.

The instant he does that, I come. My entire body wrenches into a contorted position even as he keeps pounding into me and his mouth stays latched onto my neck. The scorching heat of my orgasm sets my heart to thrashing in my chest, and my ears start to ring. Just as my climax fades, he thrusts into me one last time and howls while his release explodes inside my body and his cock pulsates.

Does it always feel this way when a man comes? Or are his climaxes more powerful because he's a werewolf? I don't care, and it doesn't matter.

He releases my neck and rests his chin on my shoulder, breathing hard.

I suck in big breaths, forcing myself to exhale slowly so I won't hyperventilate. My arms and legs are trembling.

Nathaniel pulls out of my body and repositions us so he's lying on the ground on his back and I'm sprawled on top of him. Then he combs his fingers through my hair. "Are you all right?"

"Yes, I'm fine."

Sweat glistens on our bodies, but yeah, I'm good. Beyond good, actually. What we just did has to be the most incredible sex in history. Sure, I've never been with anyone else, but I intuitively know this was mind-blowing.

I sigh and nestle my cheek against his shoulder. "Are you going to turn back into a wolf now?"

"Yes, I think so." He kisses the top of my head. "Did I hurt you? I'm fairly certain I bit you."

"It was more like you latched onto my neck. Your teeth didn't even scratch me."

"This has never happened to me before."

"Which part? The earth-shattering sex or the neck-latching?"

"Both." He hugs me to him. "I'm sorry. Once again, I neglected to consider the consequences of taking you without a French letter. You might be, ah..."

"Pregnant? Yeah, it's a possibility." I lift my head to gaze into his eyes. "I wasn't thinking about a condom either. All I cared about was being with you."

"I've never become human again after transforming while the full moon is high." He stares at me like he can't believe what he's seeing. "You made that possible."

"The medallion did it. But you're the one who showed me what I needed to do so you could un-transform."

He glances away and clears his throat. "You should prepare for me to transform again. I feel the call rising within me."

Nathaniel wriggles out from under me to kneel on the ground. He shuts his eyes and takes slow, deliberate breaths.

I pull my clothes on as fast as I can and position myself a few yards away from him.

"Hold it right there or I'll blow yer head clean off."

A sensation like an army of ice-cold ants skittering over my body makes my skin crawl. I know that voice. I squeeze my eyes shut for half a second, then I turn to face the man who had spoken.

Silas aims the long barrel of his revolver straight at Nathaniel, though he sneers at me. "Yer comin' with me, girlie. I won ya fair and square."

I glance at the Winchester rifle, but it lies on the ground a good fifteen feet away. I can't get to it before Silas pulls the trigger.

Nathaniel growls, but not in a sexy way this time. He sounds angry, and the fearsome look on his face matches the tone of his vocalization. "Turn around and leave, Silas. You have no conception of what will happen to you otherwise."

My werewolf lover curls his fingers into his palms like claws.

Silas, being an incredibly stupid jackass, cocks his gun. "Had enough of you, Sheriff. Get ready to meet yer maker."

Nathaniel hurls himself at Silas. The two men tumble to the ground, entangled while punching and kicking at each other. The gun flies out of Silas's grasp and plops down even further away from me than where the rifle lies.

I race to the Winchester, snatch it off the ground, and swing it up to take aim. Well, I try to. The two men are moving so fast I have trouble distinguishing which arm belongs to which man. One slugs the other so hard the recipient of the blow makes a dry retching sound.

The fighting ceases.

Silas lies flat on his back, eyes bulging, grimacing and gasping.

Nathaniel staggers toward me, then veers sideways. He collapses onto all fours.

And the transformation begins. His body becomes a big blur that shimmers and roils while bones crack and melt and reshape. It takes only a few seconds, then a gorgeous gray wolf stands where Nathaniel had been.

Those few seconds prove too long.

Distracted by Nathaniel's transformation, I hadn't noticed when Silas belly-crawled across the earth to grab his revolver, or when he rolled onto his side and took aim. Subconsciously, I had noticed it in my peripheral vision. But my brain didn't process the information fast enough.

Silas pulls the trigger. The shot detonates in the air, resounding off the butte with deafening volume.

The bullet slams into Wolf Nathaniel, and he crumples.

I fire on Silas, hitting him in the gut. While he slumps on the ground, his eyes vacant, I rush over to kick the revolver far away from his body in case he's not dead. Then I race to Nathaniel. Blood oozes from a wound on his side, and he's struggling to breathe. *No, no, no.* What can I do? I'm not a doctor or a veterinarian. Should I put pressure on the wound?

Laughter echoes off the stone wall of the butte. Female laughter.

Cordelia saunters out of the darkness, completely naked, and halts near Silas's body. She gazes down at him, exhales a sardonic sigh, and shakes her head. "I meant to eat him once he'd served his purpose, but I prefer fresh meat, the sort that still has blood pumping through it. I suppose I'll settle for stripping the flesh from your body instead."

She veers her attention to me.

The red spark in her eyes shudders a chill through me. Cordelia is a werewolf, so why hasn't she transformed?

"What do you want?" I ask. "And why aren't you a wolf?"

She raises her arms above her head, stretching her whole body, and sighs again—with pleasure this time. "I imagine poor Nathaniel is a slave to the moon's call, whereas I have full control over my transformations. He simply lacks the inner fortitude to become a true werewolf. As for what I want..." She bares her teeth, and her canines glisten in the moonlight. "To eat you, child, that's what I want."

I target the rifle on her. "Think again, wolf-girl."

And I pull the trigger.

The shot booms with earsplitting volume, but Cordelia is gone. She took off so fast she disappeared into the night a split second before I fired.

Fantastic. A crazy she-werewolf is running around out there, in the dark, with wolfie eyes that let her see in the dark. Me? I'm stuck with normal eyes and no frigging idea where Cordelia has gone.

Wolf Nathaniel whimpers. His eyes drift closed.

Is he dying? No, no, no, I have to save him. But how? I lean over to lay my cheek on his shoulder, and the medallion brushes my skin.

You will need its power soon, keeper of the wolf's destiny.

The old shaman's voice whispers those words in my mind, and suddenly, I know what I need to do. I clutch the medallion, shut my eyes, and pray for Nathaniel not to die. Energy sizzles over my skin. I gasp as the heat sweeps down my body with a sensation like a thousand tiny needles pricking my flesh.

The energy rushes out of me, and I look down at Wolf Nathaniel.

His wound is gone. Not just healed, but gone as if it had never existed. His eyes are still closed, though. And he's no longer a wolf, but a man again.

A shadow distends over me from behind.

"Thank you ever so much for healing him," Cordelia says. "I need Nathaniel alive in order for my plan to unfold properly."

Before I can react to the fact she's behind me, Cordelia seizes my throat and hoists me off the ground. I dangle from the hand she has fisted around my neck, tight enough that I can't shake free of her but not so tight that I choke. She has her arm raised above her head.

The ground is two feet beneath my boots.

Cordelia smiles with all the ravenous glee of a demon. "I've waited a long time for this moment, and you play a role in my plan." She opens her mouth wide. "I am starved, you see. And it's time to devour your flesh."

She slams me down on the ground. Stars burst in my vision as pain ricochets through my body.

Cordelia transmutes into a wolf in one second flat—and her open mouth descends on me.

CHAPTER TWENTY

Nathaniel

VICIOUS SNARLING REVERBERATES AROUND ME AS I ROUSE FROM UN-consciousness, blinking my eyes rapidly until I can make sense of my surroundings. My sense of smell returns first, and I sniff the air, detecting a foul odor I've smelled before. *Cordelia*. When my mind finally begins to process what I'm seeing, everything seems to unfold at a slower speed than normal, as if time itself has decelerated.

A black wolf crouches over Kylie, trapping her on the ground. The beast lowers its fangs toward her throat.

Kylie seems dazed.

I leap up and run toward Kylie and the black beast, seizing the looser skin on the back of the wolf's neck, then I rip the creature away from Kylie and hurl it at the wall of the butte.

The wolf slams into the rock face and flops onto the ground. The beast does not move, and its eyes are closed.

"Are you all right?" I ask Kylie as I help her sit up.

"Yeah. She knocked the breath out of me, but I'm not hurt."

I pull her into my arms, cradling her head to my chest.

The black wolf begins to rouse. Cordelia, the animal version of her, clambers to her feet and staggers half a step. A whining groan issues from her.

Kylie nods toward the beast. "That's Cordelia."

"Yes, I recognized her scent." I wrap both arms around Kylie while I glare at the wolf. "Stop this, Cordelia. I do not want to kill you, but I will if you persist in this madness."

How will I kill her? I have no weapons, and I'm in human form at the moment. That means I have no fangs or claws with which to rip her apart.

Cordelia shifts into human form. Her eyes are wild, and her mouth hangs open as she snarls and saliva drips from her lips. She seems to realize her state and wipes her mouth, then she straightens and glowers at Kylie. "Your little whore must die, Nathaniel. I am your true mate, and only when she is gone may we seal our bond."

"The only thing I want to seal is your tomb."

I rise, bringing Kylie up with me, and move in front of her. She presses her body against my backside. The medallion hanging around her neck has slipped out of her shirt and feels cool against my skin.

Kylie elevates herself onto her toes to whisper in my ear. "What are we going to do now?"

Cordelia laughs. "How precious. Your little whore still believes she can keep secrets from a wolf by whispering. Come, Nathaniel, we must mate before the full moon sets. I will allow your plaything to live if you come with me now."

She's in human form. Maybe I can snap her neck.

Kylie snatches something off the ground, then buries her face against my shoulder and mutters words I can't understand.

I tense, preparing to close my fist around Cordelia's throat and crush it.

The world spins around us, vanishes for half a heartbeat, and then the whirling gradually slows until we stand on solid ground with no sensation of motion. The moon's glow casts the world in false daylight, so I can tell exactly where we are.

We're standing on the street in front of the saloon.

"How did this happen?" I ask, talking to myself more than to Kylie.

But she answers. "I kind of, um, wished for us to be somewhere else, away from Cordelia. And it just...happened."

I turn toward her. "That's impossible."

She drops the rifle on the ground and plants one hand on her hip. Even in the surreal moonglow, I can tell she's giving me an exasperated look. "Turning into a werewolf isn't impossible, but me teleporting us is. That makes no sense."

"Perhaps it doesn't make sense, but I've lived with being a werewolf for five years. It's what I am." I rub my forehead, feeling a headache trying to sprout there. "I'm having a devil of a time grasping the concepts of time travel and—what was that word you said?—teleporting."

"Yeah, and that word means you disappear from one place and magically reappear somewhere else." She lays a hand on my chest. "Don't worry. You'll get used to the weirdness, eventually."

"I'm not at all certain of that."

"Trust me. If I can get used to sleeping with a werewolf, you can get used to me teleporting us with the medallion's help." She eyes me up and down. "Think we better get you some clothes and then get the hell out of Dodge."

"What does that mean?"

"Haven't you heard of Dodge City, Kansas? People needed to get out of there fast because it was a dangerous place."

"I see." Since meeting Kylie, I've learned that even if I don't understand her references, it's best to pretend I do. "We cannot leave the Outlands. Whatever or whoever created this place doesn't want anyone to escape."

"Hmm. I wonder about that."

Perhaps I wonder too, though I never had before she arrived. "We must make haste to the saloon, so I can find clothing."

I stalk down the street without waiting for Kylie, though a quick glance over my shoulder assures me she's following.

She trots to catch up to me. "After you cover up your nakedness, are we going to try leaving the Outlands? I really think we should."

"And go where?"

"This is your century. You tell me."

"I will think about it."

She makes a derisive noise. "Which means 'shut up, you annoying child, because I have no idea.' Isn't that the gist of it?"

"Perhaps. But you have no idea either, do you?"

"No. We're kinda screwed, aren't we? By the way, that means we're in big trouble."

I halt, my gaze drawn to the darkness bleeding across the sky from the direction of the Kevitash butte. The mass resembles clouds, but I've never seen a cloud as dark as the one approaching the town right now. It grows much faster than it should if it were natural, roiling and blackening as it rushes ever closer.

"What is that?" Kylie asks, her voice breathless.

"I wish I knew."

Grabbing her hand, I run toward the saloon while dragging Kylie after me. The coal-dark mass churning in the sky looms larger and nearer with every passing second. Whatever it is, I'm certain we should not be outdoors when it reaches the town.

Halfway to the saloon, I stop. Kylie bumps into me.

The townsfolk have come out of hiding. They block the doorways of all the buildings and take up positions along the porches too, ensuring we cannot escape into those structures.

At the far end of the street, a hunched figure limps toward us.

Where can we go? What should we do? I have no bloody idea, but I must protect Kylie at all costs. She is the only innocent in this town, the only one of us who has never taken a life without just cause. When she had killed Silas, the man gave her ample provocation.

Maybe I hadn't killed Cordelia after all, but my sins are numerous. Kylie believes I'm a good man. Her faith makes me wish I could believe it too.

The limping figure staggers ever closer, and the man's face comes into view.

Silas.

"I killed him," Kylie says, her tone almost panicked. "I shot him. He can't be—I mean, seriously? Werewolves are real, but come on, zombies too? This is way too much. I'm so not ready for dead people to climb out of their graves."

She's standing beside me, and I push her behind me as if I can protect her that way.

The creature that once was Silas halts a dozen yards away. The wound in his gut, where Kylie had shot him, is clearly visible and still bleeding. I might accept that Silas survived the injury, if not for his blood-red eyes and the saliva streaming from his lips. His skin has turned ashen too.

"Master wants you," Silas says, his voice rough and wheezing.

What master does he serve now?

My gaze darts to the cloud—or rather, the roiling mass of blackness. Bolts of shimmering silver lance through the cloud, and thunder rumbles overhead. Icy sweat beads on my brow. I don't feel ashamed of my fear, not this time. Anyone who is not a demonic lunatic would feel afraid in the face of such darkness.

"Give him the girl," Silas rasps. "She's his now."

The only way I will ever hand Kylie over to Silas or whatever creature he serves is if I am lying dead on the ground.

A black wolf lopes down the street toward us. The beast—Cordelia, I'm sure—stops beside Silas.

The townsfolk begin to chant in unison, their voices a chorus of monotones. "He comes. He comes. He comes."

Above us, the black cloud blots out the night sky, save for a circular hole through which the full moon gleams.

Cordelia shifts into human form in the blink of an eye, standing naked on the street. "Nathaniel, darling, do as the master asks. It will be much more enjoyable to mate with a wolf who has all his limbs intact, but I will manage even if you are torn limb from limb."

"To what vile creature have you allied yourself?" I ask.

She grins, but it's an expression of gleeful hatred, not happiness. "You'll find out soon enough. He will join us at any moment."

"How did you escape from your cell?" Though it must seem unimportant now, to everyone else, I need to know.

"Silas fired his weapon at the lock, and it shattered. You really should have stronger security measures in your jail, darling."

In the space between us and Cordelia, and the rancid Silas, the ground begins to tremble and dissolve, the liquid earth rising up, distending until it stretches into a shape reminiscent of a human body. Little by little, the vague form solidifies and mutates into a being who resembles a man, though his skin bears a slight reddish tint and his eyes are black as pitch. But yes, the creature is male. I have no doubts about that since I can see a massive bulge inside the leather trousers he wears, which mold to his body. Aside from heavy black boots, he has no other clothing on his body.

The being has a chest large enough and muscular enough to make the Greek gods envious.

"May I introduce our master," Cordelia says. "Lord Zor'imuth, King of the Demon Hordes."

"I thought Zor'imuth was a prince," Kylie says.

The red-skinned creature swerves his gaze to her and smiles with rapacious delight. "You are the Daughter of Erosabel. Are you not?"

His voice is like nothing I've ever heard, deep and resonant, rife with power.

"What if I am?" Kylie asks, peeking around my body to see the creature.

"Then you belong to me." The demon takes two steps toward us, narrowing the gap to an arm's length. "I was a prince, little one, but that was in ages past. The throne passed to me after I beheaded and consumed my father."

"I thought you got turned into a human when Erosabel cursed you."

Zor'imuth glances at Cordelia. "Is this one always so inquisitive?"

"Yes, I gather she is."

The wolf within me dislikes this conversation as much as I do. I can't stop the low growl that reverberates through my chest. "Stop speaking to Kylie. Whatever you want to say, you can direct it at me."

Cordelia exhales a melodramatic sigh. "Honestly, Nathaniel, you are in the presence of a king. Behave accordingly."

"This demon is not my master. And why has he resurrected Silas? I assume this creature is responsible for that."

"I am," Zor'imuth says, lifting his chin and rolling his shoulders back. "But why I did so is beyond the scope of your puny mortal mind." The demon glances over his shoulder at Silas. "The undead can be useful, but they give off the most noxious odors. I have no need of him now since he has completed his task by delivering my message and distracting you."

The demon waves a hand.

Silas crumples to the ground like a sack of grain.

Zor'imuth scans the length and breadth of my body. "I can see why Cordelia covets you. Go with her now and make her with child."

"No."

"You dare defy me?" He clucks his scarlet-red tongue, shaking his head slightly. "It's time to teach this wolf a lesson in obedience."

He points a finger at my chest and flicks it.

I'm hurled backward, flipping onto my stomach several feet from where Kylie and I had stood. Her eyes are wide, and her face has gone pale. I want to shout for her to run, but it will do no good. The Outlands obeys this creature, and I can feel the barriers around the town have been fortified with the demon king's magics.

He moves closer to Kylie, though he doesn't touch her. His rapacious gaze sweeps over her, and he groans. "You will make a fine queen, and I will enjoy ravaging your body. To defile a Daughter of Erosabel is the sweetest revenge for what that harpy did to me. Was it so horrible for her in my kingdom? I offered her the pleasure of lying with me every night, but rather than thanking me, the wench tried to escape. I hunted her down, of course. No one takes my property."

Kylie holds perfectly still, as if she fears any movement might anger the demon. "I thought Erosabel turned you into a human. A werewolf, but a mortal man."

"Oh yes, she did." He clenches his teeth. "The little witch."

"But you're a demon again."

"Yes, I fought for centuries to regain my demonic form." He grasps her upper arm. "Enough chitchat, little one. It's time for our wedding."

"I will never marry you. Might as well kill me now."

He chuckles, the sound so dark and menacing I feel the hairs on my arms stiffening. "Did I say you had a choice?"

I try to get up, but my body seems glued to the ground. If that bastard touches Kylie, if he so much as scratches her cheek, I will find a way to free myself and tear his head off his body.

Zor'imuth looks at Cordelia. "Take your pathetic mate and leave us."

Kylie straightens, and I recognize the expression on her face. She has summoned her stubborn side, the part of her personality that inspired me to growl at her often—but also convinced me she is the only woman I want.

"May I know one thing first?" Kylie asks. "If I promise to go with you willingly after you tell me what I want to know."

She can't honestly mean to go with him. It's a trick of some sort.

Zor'imuth rolls his eyes. "If you must."

"How did you un-curse yourself?"

The demon waves for Cordelia to approach him, though he keeps his hold on Kylie's arm. "Why don't you enlighten her?"

My former fiancée smiles with no small measure of smugness. "When I devoured the gypsy hag, her magics flowed into me. I went on to devour several of her kinfolk, thus acquiring their power too. I heeded the call, just like Nathaniel, but mine came from a different source. Whereas he followed the path laid out by the Daughters of Erosabel, I sought the demon prince who had enslaved her. The power that had once flowed within him was far greater than anything humans possess. When I removed his curse, he became a demon once again, and in gratitude to me, he offered to help me find Nathaniel."

Zor'imuth leans in, his face inches from Kylie's. "Cordelia told me she'd sniffed out a Daughter of Erosabel and that she could lead me to you. And that is the story. As for the ending..." He seizes Kylie's shoulders and pulls her into him. "I now possess the Rom witch's last descendant."

"I'm curious about something," Kylie says. "Did you create the ironclad room above the saloon?"

"Of course. I needed to contain your lover until Cordelia and I completed our plans. Couldn't have him destroying the Outlands, so a key was given to the saloon owner so she could confine at night."

He's referring to Lucy. The demon king must not know she gave me the key, which means he's not quite as clever as he believes.

Kylie lowers her gaze to the demon king's loins and speaks in a sultry voice. "May I see what exactly I'm getting? Call it a preview before the wedding."

Smirking, he steps back to unhook the buttons on his leather trousers, then he pushes them down to his ankles. "Look your fill, little one."

I can't fathom what she's doing, but I pray it's part of a plan for her to escape. Struggle as I might, I cannot break free of the invisible barrier pinning me to the ground.

"Wow, you are hung," Kylie says as she splays a hand on the demon's lower belly. "May I touch you?"

"Yes, of course. This will be inside you soon enough."

Kylie slides her hand down to his loins and narrows her gaze on Zor'imuth. "I don't think so, asshat."

She clamps her hand around his bollocks and wrenches them.

Zor'imuth wails, stumbling backward while cupping his loins.

My testicles hurt just watching what Kylie did.

She pulls the medallion out of her shirt and clutches it in her fist. Shutting her eyes, she twists her features into a grimace as if she's struggling to accomplish something.

Wind gyrates around us, tossing her hair and flinging grit into my eyes. I try to clear my gaze by blinking and rubbing my eyes, but the wind whips dust into the air and obscures my view even more.

A woman's scream rips through the air, deafening and unearthly.

Zor'imuth wails again, louder than before, and the cry goes on and on.

The wind fades away. The sky above is clear, the moon hanging lower to the horizon.

Kylie stands before Zor'imuth, seeming dazed, while the demon king collapses to his knees. His red skin has become a natural shade of tan, and his eyes have taken on a brown, human color.

"What have you done?" Zor'imuth bellows.

"Nothing," Kylie says, stumbling backward. "Erosabel did it, through me. She made you mortal, for real and for good this time. You're not a demon or a werewolf, just an average human."

A flash of movement draws my attention to something past Kylie.

Cordelia has dropped to her hands and knees. In a flash, she transforms into a wolf and leaps at Kylie.

I scramble to my feet and snare the rifle, raising it to fire a single shot.

The round strikes the black wolf between the eyes.

And the beast crumples to the ground. The wolf melts back into Cordelia, who lies lifeless in the dirt.

I push past the mewling former demon and pull Kylie into my arms, hugging her to me like she might fly away into the sky if I let go.

She wraps her arms around me. "Is Cordelia dead?"

"Most likely, but I need to be certain this time."

Reluctantly, I release Kylie and kneel beside Cordelia, holding a hand beneath her nostrils to feel for breath. I feel nothing, so I hold a finger to her inner wrist, but I can't detect her heartbeat there. "She's dead."

Kylie holds out her hand to me. "We need to get out of here."

I take her hand, rising. "Why? Cordelia is gone, and the demon king is no longer a threat."

"Yeah, but I'm pretty sure he created the Outlands. And I don't think it's going to be happy about what's happened."

"The Outlands is not a living being."

"No, but I think it is living magic." She shifts her attention to Zor'imuth, who has stopped wailing and now stares blankly at the ground. "You created the Outlands, didn't you?"

He nods weakly.

"Is it bound to you by magic?" she asks. "Will the Outlands disappear now?"

Zor'imuth raises his head, revealing his haggard expression. "Yes, it will. And there is nothing you can do to escape. The greatest evil will consume this town and all of us with it."

I hear a distant rumbling and ask Zor'imuth, "What is coming?"

"The end of us all." He tries to smile but gives up. "Every living thing in the Outlands, every being who was consigned here with good cause, will be destroyed in the most painful way possible. And there's nothing you can do to stop it."

Kylie glares at him. "Like hell there isn't."

The rumbling grows louder, barreling toward us faster than any wind or tornado could travel. But it's not a tidal wave or a sandstorm. An invisible force bears down on us, and the barrier that confines the Outlands refuses to let us leave.

Screams resound through the town as men and women alike are torn to shreds, their remains disintegrating before our eyes.

"You cannot escape!" Zor'imuth bellows.

Kylie throws her arms around me, the medallion trapped between our chests, and squeezes me so tightly I can't breathe.

The world gyrates around us.

Silence overtakes the world for a heartbeat, then I hear the rustle of a light wind.

Peeling my eyelids apart, I scan our surroundings but can't understand what I'm seeing. We seem to be standing at the edge of town. The sun blazes down on us, and strange people dressed in strange clothing amble down the street, gazing around with mild curiosity. The buildings look different. They seem...older and yet also newer.

A sign a few yards to our left calls this "Wrathrock, Utah's Famous Ghost Town."

Wrathrock? I recognize the buildings, though they've changed, so I know this is the unnamed town in the Devil's Outlands.

Something growls and roars further down the street, though I can't see what it is.

An enormous rectangular box fitted with large black wheels rolls down the street toward us.

"Mom, look!" a child cries out. "That guy's naked!"

Kylie grabs my hand and takes a step back. "I think we better get out of sight and find you some clothes before you get arrested."

"I am the sheriff. Do you think I'll arrest myself?"

"No, but, uh..." She bites her lip. "We're not in the town you knew anymore. I'll explain after we get you dressed."

"Kylie!" a woman shouts. "Girl, where have you been? Are you okay?"

The woman, who has just emerged from the nearest building, rushes toward us.

She's clothed in what looks like undergarments, scraps of fabric not much larger than what Kylie had been wearing when I'd first seen her. This girl seems to be wearing lavender knickers that barely cover her arse and a shirt that barely covers her bosom.

The girl throws her arms around Kylie. "We've been worried sick about you."

"I'm fine, Jenna," Kylie says. "I swear it. You can stop crushing me now."

Jenna releases Kylie, then she seems to notice me for the first time. Her gaze travels over me from head to toe—twice. Her lips curve into a sly smirk. "Damn, Kylie, you need to take me wherever you went. If they make naked hotties like him over there, I'll be moving to that place tomorrow."

Hotties? I assume that's somehow related to "hot," the word Kylie likes to use.

The rectangular conveyance I'd seen a moment ago rolls past us, and I see men, women, and children inside it.

"What the devil is that?" I ask.

Kylie pats my shoulder. "Let's call it a horseless carriage for now. I'll explain the rest later."

"Where the blazes are we?"

"Not where, Nathaniel. When."

CHAPTER TWENTY-ONE

Kylie

POOR NATHANIEL. HE LOOKS SO COMPLETELY OVERWHELMED AND BE-wildered that I want to hug him and kiss him, but we need to get him some clothes first. I wonder how nineteenth-century people would react to a gorgeous naked man appearing out of nowhere on the street. Modern people have mixed reactions. Some of the tourists seem shocked, others try not to smile, and a few don't seem to notice at all.

How could anyone fail to notice Nathaniel Fortescue in the nude? I mean damn, that man is supernova hot.

Jenna waggles her eyebrows. "Naked and British. Wow, girl, you really hit the jackpot."

Megan sprints out of the livery stable, and when she notices me and Nathaniel, she shrieks and hightails it over here. Breathing hard, she gives me a lopsided grin. "We've been looking everywhere for you. What happened?"

Something profoundly weird that's impossible to explain. For my two best friends, I'll have to try. But not out here on the street.

Megan swerves her attention to Nathaniel, skimming her gaze up and down his nude body. "Holy shit, hon, where'd you find this guy?" Her eyes flare wide, and her jaw drops. "Oh God, did he rape you?"

"No, no, it's nothing like that. This is Nathaniel Fortescue. He's a good man, but the how and why of everything is a long story." I tip my head toward the British werewolf. "First, we need to get him dressed before somebody calls the cops."

"Oh, yeah. Sure, babe, I'll go to the general store and grab something. Jenna, why don't you come with me?"

"We'll wait for you guys behind this building." The sign above it calls this Sassy May's Boarding House, which I remember from the tour the other day. Or maybe that was today. Not sure how this timeline meshes with the one from eighteen ninety-three.

My two friends jog off down the street.

Nathaniel stares up at the sign on the building as I usher him around the structure to the area behind it where tourists don't seem to go. Nobody out there can see us back here.

"Why is this building called Sassy May's Boarding House?" he asks. "There is no such establishment in the Outlands. This building houses the solicitor's office. He lives on the second floor."

"Yeah, I know. But that was then, and this is now."

"I don't understand."

"Remember what I said about time travel?" I hunch my shoulders and spread my hands. "Well, it happened again. Only this time, I kinda did it on purpose without knowing how I did that. I wished for us to be somewhere safe, and the medallion granted my request."

"How are we safe with so many people wandering about?"

"No demons or whackjob were-bitches around here, as far as I know."

Two ATVs come roaring up the dirt road into town, jouncing over a pothole, and the riders whoop and laugh.

Nathaniel's eyes bulge, and his jaw goes slack. "What the bloody hell is that?"

"Maybe your lesson in modern transportation should wait until later." I slip my arms around his waist and rest my chin on his chest to look up at him. "You're in the twenty-first century now, Lord Wilderhampton."

"This is your world? I don't understand how you can live in a place as noisy and bizarre as this."

I pat his chest. "Yeah, that's pretty much how I felt when I crash-landed in the Outlands."

Jenna and Megan trot around the corner of the building toward us. Megan has bottles of water and bags of junk food in her arms while Jenna cradles a bag of what looks like clothes. They're both breathing hard, like they ran all the way here from the store.

My friends blatantly ogle Nathaniel while he gets dressed.

He makes a series of faces while he does that, everything from annoyed to baffled and even amused.

Well, he is wearing a T-shirt that features Bugs Bunny dressed as a cowboy. My favorite part of his ensemble, however, is the tight, low-slung jeans my friends picked for him. I don't wonder how they chose the right sizes for Nathaniel, since Jenna has always had a great eye for that.

Even in a goofy T-shirt, Nathaniel is sexy as hell.

"I feel ridiculous," he announces. "Is this truly how men of this era dress?"

"Not all of them," I say. "Some wear even dumber clothes."

Megan nudges me with her elbow. "Where have you been hiding this stud muffin? Thought you didn't have a boyfriend."

I didn't. Not the last time I saw them. Whether Nathaniel wants to be my boyfriend is another question. But I inform my friends, "I need to tell you guys a long story that you may not believe, but I swear it's all true. Let's catch a ride back to Fiara Flats, and I promise I'll explain everything."

Luckily, we don't have to wait long for the next stagecoach back to Fiara Flats. People are still looking at Nathaniel askance, probably remembering he'd been stark naked a little while ago. We have the stagecoach to ourselves—just me, my werewolf, and my best friends. Jenna and Megan jabber the whole time, but they don't quiz Nathaniel, not yet. They seem to realize he's kind of confused right now, so they cut him some slack.

Once we get back to the hotel, my friends get busy ordering pizza for lunch, which involves lots of haggling over what toppings to choose. While they're busy, I lead Nathaniel over to the corner by the window, farthest from Jenna and Megan.

"How are you doing with the time-traveling and the modern world?" I ask. "Must be confusing for you."

"It is, but I will adapt. Adjusting to becoming a werewolf was far more confusing."

"Yeah, I imagine it was."

Okay, I don't need to worry about Nathaniel. At least, not in terms of dealing with a bizarre new world. A werewolf can handle that.

After I relate the entire bizarre story to my friends, I expect them to think I'm insane and abduct me to a psychiatric clinic. But they don't freak out. I swear to them it's true, and Nathaniel backs me up, so they accept that we believe that's what happened. Jenna and Megan can't come up with any alternate explanations for my missing time and my eighteen-hour disappearance, and they know I wouldn't lie.

Yeah, I was gone for eighteen hours. It felt like a lot longer to me.

Whether they accept my story as fact, I don't know. My friends are too kind to tell me so if they think it's bullshit.

Life must go on, though, and I have a lot to teach Nathaniel about my world.

Jenna and Megan share an apartment near the university, but luckily, I've got my own pad not far from their building. I think Nathaniel needs time away from my friends while he gets used to the modern world. Cell phones completely befuddle him. And don't even get me started on TVs and Bluetooth ear thingies. Cars don't bother him too much once he gets used to the noise and the lack of large animals pulling them.

As for modern slang... Let's not even go there.

Nathaniel and I haven't had sex since the night Cordelia and the demon king captured us. I think he worries about what our previous liaisons might have done to me, in terms of pregnancy and other things, like whether he could turn me into a werewolf that way. There won't be another full moon for three weeks, so we have to wait and see.

The full moon comes and goes, but I do not develop a thick coat of body hair or a ravenous hunger for blood. Nathaniel and I agree that means sex with him did not turn me into a werewolf. He doesn't shapeshift either on that night, and he hasn't needed to run free either, but I can't convince him he's not a wolf anymore. Nathaniel insists it's just a reprieve, not a permanent change, though he can't explain how or why that might've happened.

A week later, while we're enjoying Chinese takeout in our apartment, Nathaniel sets his carton of lo mein on the coffee table and turns toward me. "May I see the medallion?"

"Uh, sure." I've been wearing it around my neck, hidden under my shirt, so I pull it out and hold it up for him to see. "Are you looking for something?"

He touches his fingertip to the medallion, holding it there for several seconds, then he wraps his hand around it.

"You're not on fire," I say. "Guess the medallion finally decided it likes you."

"Perhaps." He lets go of the bronze disk. "I've been having dreams about the past, about what happened to us and what I've left behind, unfinished."

"What are you saying?"

"In my dreams, the medallion takes me back to my time." He squirms and scratches his cheek. "And I, ah, think that's what I need to do. To make certain Cordelia and Zor'imuth truly are dead, and to settle things at Wilderhampton."

"Settle things? I don't understand."

"You will." He stands up. "I need to go now."

"Right this second?" I jump up, shaking my head furiously. "No, you can't, please. What if there's no way back?"

"I need to make certain you will be cared for, no matter what happens to me." He clasps my hands. "Please understand, Kylie, I don't want to be away from you. But I cannot leave the past unsettled."

"Take me with you."

"I need to know you are safe, here in your own time. Please believe me, I do not wish to leave you, and I will move heaven and earth to return to you. But I need to do this."

My eyes have started to sting, and I know I'll cry any second. I bow my head, so he won't see my tears. My throat is tight too, and I feel a little nauseous.

He touches a fingertip to the underside of my chin and lifts it until I have to look at him. "I will come back to you, I vow it. But I have no idea how long it might take, if I can return to this moment or if more time must pass before I find you again."

I nod while tears stream down my cheeks.

Nathaniel enfolds me in his arms and kisses my forehead. He holds me for a moment, then steps back.

I wipe my eyes, stand up straight, and hand him the medallion. "Do what you need to do. I'll wait for as long as it takes."

He closes his fist around the medallion and vanishes.

And I cry for the better part of three days. Then I suck it up and go back to living my life, as best I can when the man I love has disappeared into the past. Yeah, I realized I love him a nanosecond after he vanished. He doesn't even know how I feel.

Two weeks later, I rent an ATV and head back toward Wrathrock, though I don't stop there. I ride out to the Kevitash butte, and armed with a battery-powered lantern, I make my way down the hidden passageway into the cavern where Nathaniel and I had first made love. He's not here, of course. I set the lantern down and approach the paintings.

"I wondered how long it would take you to come here."

The voice is familiar, but it's not Nathaniel. I turn toward the old shaman.

He hobbles closer, gripping his walking stick. "You feel great sadness. I sense it in you, but there is hope."

"Are you saying Nathaniel will come back?"

"I haven't come to issue prophecies, dear." He moves even closer and stretches out a hand to clasp mine. "You are not the last descendant of Erosabel, but you are the one who broke the curse and freed the wolf. He is no longer what he was, but he has become what he should be."

"What does that mean?"

"You will see." He approaches the wall, lifting a bony finger to trace the lines in the paintings. "I've done what Erosabel bade me to do, and it's time I ascend to the spirit world. I've waited a thousand years for this day." He smiles at me. "Thank you, dear. You have freed me too. Be well, and do not fear for the future."

He disappears, and his clothing slumps to the floor. The walking stick thumps down beside his clothes.

The paintings vanish too.

I don't even try to understand what happened that day.

Two months after he left, I get some news that confirms my conviction I will wait as long as it takes for Nathaniel to return. What else can I do? We're connected in so many ways that no one else could ever fill the void.

Months roll by, one bleeding into the next, while I await Nathaniel's return. He vowed he would find a way, and I believe in him more than anyone else in the world, in any timeline. His absence creates an ache in my soul that will never go away unless he comes back to me. Maybe I'm not miserable every moment of every day, but I think about him that often. Think and pray and dream of him.

Before I know it, I've finished my master's degree. But instead of becoming an ornithologist, I get a job working at Wrathrock Ghost Town as a tour guide, mostly because I have the strangest intuition that when Nathaniel returns, he'll turn up here. People love my tall tales about a British cowboy and the town he tamed. It's only part fiction. I based most of it on Nathaniel and the Outlands gang. My friends and my parents must think I'm crazy, but they support me anyway. Yeah, I told my parents all about my adventure in the past. No idea if they believe it one hundred percent, but they know I'm not lying.

On the one-year anniversary of the day I was catapulted into the past, I'm sitting on the steps of the saloon watching the tourists go by.

A figure emerges from behind the livery stable and saunters toward me.

My heart stutters. I leap up, squinting in the bright sunlight, and a tingle shivers over my skin from head to toe. Oh God, is it really...

"Nathaniel!" I shriek.

And I race across the street, hurling myself at him.

CHAPTER TWENTY-TWO

Nathaniel

KYLIE FLINGS HER ENTIRE BODY AT ME, LASHING HER ARMS AROUND my neck while her feet dangle six inches off the ground. I hug her to me, burying my face in her hair, inhaling the scent of her that I've missed for so long.

"Please let go of me," I say. "I need to look at you, love."

She slides down my body until her feet touch the ground. Her gaze wanders over me from my face to my feet and back again. "You look different."

I'm wearing a grey suit, fashioned from tweed, with a matching waistcoat and a black four-in-hand tie, not to mention shiny black shoes. Perhaps I am a bit overdressed for a ghost town that serves as a tourist attraction. Kylie is wearing white shorts and a pink T-shirt with flowers embroidered on it. I love her in that outfit. And yes, I'd learned some of the modern clothing terminology before I went back to the nineteenth century.

"Is my clothing too much?" I ask. "I wanted to look my best when I came home to you."

"Maybe it's a teeny bit much, but you look smokin' hot in that suit." She grasps my face and kisses me. "I'm so glad you're back. I missed you like crazy."

"I missed you too, more than words can convey." I pull her into my arms, and she sets her palms on my chest while she gazes up at me with a loving expression. I brush a lock of hair away from her eyes. "I took care of everything. Cordelia and Zor'imuth are gone, as is everyone who was consigned to the Outlands. It's over, for good."

She rests her forehead on my chest and sighs. "Thank goodness."

"And I settled things at Wilderhampton too."

Kylie lifts her head. "What did you do? Burn it down?"

"No. I decided to save it. Just because my father was an evil bastard doesn't mean the house is evil." I tug her more firmly against me, needing as much contact as possible after so long away from her. "Why should I let the Crown take the entire estate? With my uncles gone, there is no one else to inherit. Except for me."

"So you reclaimed your title and estate? You're Lord Wilderhampton again?"

"Yes. But I didn't do it exclusively for me." I touch my lips to her forehead. "My wife will share my good fortune, as will any children we have."

"Oh really." She gives me a sly smile. "Who did you marry?"

"No one, yet." I take half a step back and take her hands, holding them between us. "I love you, Kylie, so very much. Will you do me the honor of becoming my wife?"

She grins. "Yes, of course. And I love you too. God, do I love you."

I pull an item out of my pocket and hold it out to her. "This ring belonged to my grandmother, and my mother gave it to me with the command that I must give it to my wife." I slip the ring, with its small garnet stone, onto Kylie's finger. "I'm sure she is watching over us and is overjoyed that I finally claimed my rightful inheritance and found the perfect woman."

"Your mom would be proud of you, for sure." Kylie bites her upper lip. "There's something I need to tell you. I hope it won't shock your Victorian sensibilities."

"I used to be a werewolf, love. I can handle whatever you need to say."

She opens her mouth as if to speak, then shuts it. Her head tilts to the side, and her gaze narrows. "What do you mean you 'used to be' a werewolf? Thought you were convinced you would become one again, eventually."

"The events of that night, when Zor'imuth arrived, changed me. I have finally accepted that fact, since I've been through several lunar cycles without experiencing the slightest need to transform or consume blood." I cup her cheek in one hand. "When you broke the curse, you freed me. I am a normal man."

"You were probably still a wolf when you knocked me up, but the baby seems totally normal too."

"Knocked up?" I glance down at her flat belly. "Baby?"

"Yeah, 'knocked up' means I was pregnant. Your daughter was born three months ago." She nods toward the saloon. "Wanna come upstairs and meet her? Jenna babysits for me when I'm working on Saturdays."

All I can do is splutter and grin like an idiot.

Kylie leads me into the saloon and upstairs to the iron-clad bedroom, swinging the door open.

Her friend Jenna is rocking a baby in her arms while humming softly. When she sees us, she leaps up and squeals. "He came back! Oh, Kylie, I'm so happy for you guys."

Jenna rushes over to hand me the baby.

I gingerly accept the precious package, gazing down into eyes the same color as mine. My daughter. I have a child, and she is beautiful and perfect just like her mother.

Jenna leaves and shuts the door.

"What is she called?" I ask.

"Charlotte, after your mother."

I kiss the babe's forehead, overcome by an emotion I never imagined I would experience—love for my child and my soon-to-be wife. I have a family.

"Just curious," Kylie says. "How can you inherit Wilderhampton if you're living in the twenty-first century?"

"A Rom elder visited me not long after I returned to England. We had a long and interesting discussion about the curse one of their own laid down on me." I walk over to the bed and settle onto it, but I can't tear my gaze away from my daughter, snuggled in my arms. "The elder assured me the Rom would take care of giving me an identity in this century. There should be a birth certificate on file for me in England, or whatever the modern version of my homeland is now called, and there will also be documentation of Fortescue heirs in the generations that succeeded me. No one has ever seen them, naturally, since they prefer to live in South America."

"But, um, how could the Rom guarantee all that?"

I lift my gaze to Kylie. "How do you think? They used their magics, love."

"Of course." She sits down on the bed beside me. "So, are we moving to England?"

"That's entirely up to you. I can claim my inheritance but live here in America." I slide my free arm around Kylie. "It's your decision. I know very little about this world."

"Let's play it by ear. First, you need to meet my parents."

I can't help grimacing. "What will they think of me? I abandoned you for...how long?"

"A year."

"You had a child out of wedlock. I can't imagine what your family must think of—"

She seals my lips with two fingers. "Shush, Nathaniel. This is the twenty-first century, and these days, lots of women have babies without getting married. I've told my parents all about you. They'll love you, honey, trust me."

I do trust her, and I owe her everything. She saved my life and my soul. I will repay that debt the only way I can—by loving her forever.

"Perhaps I'm not a werewolf any longer," I say, "but I may occasionally growl like one."

She leans in close, her lips grazing mine. "You damn well better. Your growling makes so hot for you."

"Let's go home, wherever that may be, so I can make you hot for hours."

"Better make it days. We've got loads of missed sex to catch up on."

"I'm yours until the end of eternity, Lady Wilderhampton."

Did you love

Visit

AnnaDurand.com

to subscribe to her newsletter
for updates on forthcoming books
&
to receive exclusive content!

ANNA DURAND IS A BESTSELLING, MULTI-AWARD-WINNING AUTHOR OF contemporary and paranormal romance. Her books have earned bestseller status on every major retailer and wonderful reviews from readers around the world. But that's the boring spiel. Here are some really cool things you want to know about Anna!

Born on Lackland Air Force Base in Texas, Anna grew up moving here, there, and everywhere thanks to her dad's job as an instructor pilot. She's lived in Texas (twice), Mississippi, California (twice), Michigan (twice), and Alaska—and now Ohio.

As for her writing, Anna has always invented stories in her head, but she didn't write them down until her teen years. Those first awful books went into the trash can a few years later, though she learned a lot from those stories. Eventually, she would pen her first romance novel, the paranormal romance *Willpower*, and she's never looked back since.

To get exclusive content, join Anna's Facebook group, Anna's Romance Addicts, or sign up for her newsletter.

Visit AnnaDurand.com to sign up.

www.ingramcontent.com/pod-product-compliance
Lightning Source LLC
Chambersburg PA
CBHW071825190726

48292CB00005B/1616